Steele Creek

James McCloud
Texas Ranger

CURTIS HAWK

Copyright © 2012 Curtis Hawk

All rights reserved.

ISBN:
ISBN-13: 9781520980119

DEDICATION

To my Parents, three brothers, and two sisters
Who had past, too soon?

Ora Weldon and Barbara E. Hawk
Johnnie, Ora Jr. and Richard
Gloria and Connie.

To all the men and women who have served.

ACKNOWLEDGMENTS

To the real James McCloud, and a real honest Texan.
A Friend and Inspiration giving me a character to write about and approving the use of his name.

The real Jim McCloud is nothing like the actual character. However, I believe if he was born in the Old Texas of the 1880's he would most likely became this character and a Lawman.

Thank you James:

To the many other friends that became my characters; too many to mention here look for your name in this Novel; I thank you.

This book is a work of fiction. Names, characters, places, and incidents either are the product of my imagination or are used fictitiously, and any resemblance to actual person, living dead, businesses, companies, events, or locales is entirely coincidental.

From the James McCloud,
Texas Ranger Series

PROLOGUE

1887 Dallas Texas

James McCloud became a Texas Ranger when he was twenty years old he had grown up under the care of a family friend Abigail and her husband John MacKinnon after his mother had passed away.
John and Abigail owned the MacKinnon Hardware store in Amarillo it had been his MacKinnon's father's business before he had taken over after his fathers passing of assumption.
At the age of Twenty, James McCloud followed in his father's footsteps and became a Texas Ranger.

The man riding along the trail suddenly stopped. At first glance, it looked like any other of the tall ponderosa pines growing on the mountainside, the only difference being a slight bulge on one side. Upon closer examination, the bulge could be made out to be a man dressed in buckskins and a black vest.

Near Texarkana, Texas

To say McCloud was a big man would be an understatement. McCloud was big, a little over six feet tall in his bare feet, but he was also massive. He reminded you of a thick brown grizzly. McCloud moved with the easy grace of someone who was comfortable with himself. You got the feeling that this man was a tremendous powerhouse that was barely contained. McCloud had grown up moving huge loads of supplies while helping John McKinnon in his work in the hardware store. The large barrels of hand made nails, rolls of wire, tons of bags of grain and flour. James had grown into the strength required to move the merchandise, first unloading them from the train to the wagon, then into the back storeroom of the hardware store, finally helping their customers load the purchases they made.

Sometimes moving enough lumber to build an entire house in town His shoulders and back were layered in massive muscles that rippled like bagged snakes beneath his skin. His chest was as big as a barrel.

The rider dismounted and began walking his horse forward into the Pines as he called out, "James – James McCloud is that you?"

"That would be me, how can I help you Mister...?"

"My name is Edward Pinkerton and I was told that you would be out this way, I mean no harm and my weapons are secured."

"Come on ahead Mr. Pinkerton, but keep your hands where I can see them?"
Edward continued ahead until James stepped out from where he had been standing, he was ten feet up on the rock face tucked in between a deep crevice. Pinkerton could now see him clearly, although with the morning sun behind McCloud he was still just a large bulky shape like the rocks around him.

"Close enough I can see you are not looking for a fight, so what is it that brought you out here looking for me?"

"As I said my name is Edward Pinkerton, but please call me Ed, I am a member of the Pinkerton Family National Detective Agency. Allen Pinkerton, Founder of the agency is my elder brother?"

"Yes, the Pinkerton's I have heard of your agency. But it still does not answer as to why you would be looking for me Sir?"

"Well we have been trying to track down a man, Mr. Burl Carlington for two years now, he and two other men robbed a train east of Kansas City, Missouri they got away with over one hundred thousand in cash from the Kingston Mines payroll and several of the passengers watches and jewelry."

Edward paused then continued, "Burl and Clayton Scrim got away clean that day and Brett Grisset was killed on the train, by another one of your Texas Rangers, Bucky Washam."

"Yeah, I heard about that one the Dallas News called it the 'The Great Kingston Mines Train Robbery' the story said they tracked them south and lost track of them somewhere in the Louisiana Territory, along the swamps. By the way, Bucky Washam is now a Captain in the Rangers in Amarillo!"

Pinkerton agreed that the story was correct and added that Brett Grisset was later killed up near Amarillo. "Gunned down by a Sheriff's Deputy in a barroom brawl. Most likely over some a card game!"

"And you tracked me down, for what? Do you think I have some information that your fancy Detective Agency could not discover!"

"Well yes and no, McCloud we were hoping you would have heard something in the wind about Burl Carlington, or at least would help us in tracking him down?"

"I will telegraph the Dallas office and see if I can help you or if I might have another case pending!"

"Thank you, Ranger McCloud, I will be at the Drowning Creek boarding house, in Texarkana if you can find out today I will meet you there and buy you a Steak dinner and we can go over what we know so far?"

"I'll let you know by this evening, Mr. Pinkerton I am sorry you said to call you Ed."

CHAPTER 1

Captain Vance sent the telegraph giving James the approval to work alongside the Pinkerton's saying, "You might just learn a few new detective skills from Edward Pinkerton?"

"Most likely that is going to be the other way around they have been looking for this 'Burl Carleton' for two years now. I do not plan on spending more than a month on this one Sir!" James replied.

James met Ed Pinkerton at the Drowning Creek for dinner. The room was crowded with the evening diners who had departed the Overland stage for the evening stop. He stood in the room scanning the crowd until he noticed Pinkerton. Edward was smaller than he had looked earlier and now up close. He was dressed in a nice suit, bolo tie and was sporting his distinguished handlebar moustache. He stood as James approached his table, to James surprise he stood only five foot three inches and was slight in build but looked like he could probably handle himself if his opponent wasn't to large of a man. They again exchanged greetings and James said he had approval to help the Pinkerton's in the search for Carlington.

Dinner was served Ed had ordered for James, Carmella had brought out two large plates, James' plate had a very large T-Bone steak, medium rare grilled over an open fire and seasoned just to his liking. Ed's was quite a bit smaller but still a good size chunk of meat for such a little guy James thought.

"Well it looks as if you did your homework and found out just how I like my Steak cooked."

"I had asked around and it was Carmella here that suggested this dinner for you!"

Ed poured them each a large mug of cold beer and began eating. Carmella and her daughter LeAnn was extremely busy but had found time to stop by to see if there was any thing they needed throughout their dinner. The conversation during dinner was held to small talk as the discussed the history Pinkerton Detective Agency and that of the Texas Rangers. James had learned that the Pinkerton's had become the largest detective agency in the United States and were mostly known for breaking up conflicts with Company unionists, they had been established in 1850 by Allan Pinkerton a former Chicago Detective. Allan was Edward's uncle and he was primed to go into the business by Allen Pinkerton.

James had shared with Edward his life after his mother was murdered when he was very young and that his Father was a Texas Ranger, so therefore he also had followed his father into the business when he was Twenty years of age.

"I was brought up by a close family friend of my parents, John and Abigail MacKinnon they ran a hardware and supplies store where I worked until duty called me into law enforcement. My Father had visited me often and took me with him on trips out in the wilderness teaching me a lot about survival and life outside city limits."

After dinner was finished, they retired to the sitting room of the boarding house and sat enjoying cigars and after dinner drinks.

Edward began the discussion about the timeline and results of the search for Burl Carlington.

"The last confirmed sighting was in six months ago in Lubbock where he robbed a stage coach of its strong box and the passengers. The coach's driver and guard were shot dead and one of the passengers was beaten pretty bad, but survived."

"How was he confirmed as the robber?" asked James.

"By the wife of the man beaten, for refusing to give up his money and his wife's jewelry, identified him by the facial scar over his right eye, it is very distinctive as it curls around from his hairline and down to just above his jawbone. One of the other passengers heard the guard call him Burl he must have known him from someplace. We could not track down where he knew him from, maybe just remembered the face on a wanted poster!"

"Six month's is a long time he could have made it to Mexico or who knows west to California or east to New York?"

"You are right, but our investigations leads us to believe he has stayed here in Texas, as it is so wide open between cities of any size."

"What about other known associates, women he visits often, family known, anything?"

"No, that is why we came looking for you. You are well known as the Rangers best tracker and we hope you can pickup something we missed."

James sat creating cigar smoke rings in the air before he spoke, "Well someone has done the bragging for me so there is no use denying the fact that I am, 'The Best' at tracking the men I am assigned to find."

"Well don't hurt your self, patting your own back!" Ed said laughing.

They agreed to depart after breakfast the next morning. James said, "I am sure I could come up with a WAG by then.

Ed looked at him and had to ask, "What is a WAG?"

"Wild Ass Guess." Was his reply.

By Ten a.m., the next morning they were heading out of Texarkana heading west.

CHAPTER 2

Together they rode on up to Paris Texas. The saloon was their first stop in town, upon passing through the open double doors. James noticed the Sheriff of Paris leaning against the bar. Sheriff Thomas Bailey looked over the top of his beer mug as McCloud entered, "Well I'll be damned what in the hell brought you through here James?"

"First let's do introductions, Tom this is Edward Pinkerton, Ed this here is the famous Thomas Bailey Sheriff of Paris Texas, a place where there has never been a murder or bank robbery in the fifty years he has been Sheriff here."

"A Pinkerton Detective riding with you James?" Tom asked.

"Not just a Pinkerton Detective but Mr. Ed Pinkerton himself!"

"No Shit, his name is Pinkerton? I bet that is not just a coincidence either?"

Ed ordered a round of beers for the three of them and explained who they were looking for.
Sheriff Bailey stated that he had heard about the train robbery and the latest stage robbery, hearing that the latest had killed a man he knew. "Jake Roberts was the Guard on that Stage he was shot in the back as Burl Carlington rode up on them from behind."

James asked him, "How did you come to know Jake Roberts?"

"His Uncle was one of my Deputies fifteen years ago and young Jake would visit him in the late fall each year. Good boy he was, let's see he would have been about twenty three or four this year."

"And what about his Uncle?" asked Ed.

"Jake was named after his uncle, Deputy Jake Roberts retired after he met his wife. She came down from one of those cold states up north. Hell they are all cold, though ain't they up north. Well any way he lives just outside of town and he comes in here to the saloon every evening. Most likely within the next hour or so." Tom continued,

"Emmett Aiken over there was a good friend of young Jake when he was visiting his Uncle they hung around and went fishing and such."

"Let me go speak to him alone." said McCloud. Emmet was playing cards with a few other men when James approached them. "Mr. Aiken, my name is James McCloud, Texas Ranger could I have a few minutes of your time?"

"Sure, I have not done anything wrong have I?" Emmet asked.

"No just want to ask you a few questions about an old friend of yours Jake Roberts."

"Jake was killed in a stage robbery months ago he was a stage coach guard and one of the good guys, why are you asking about him?" Emmet looked frustrated.

"We know Jake was a good person and did not deserve to be shot in the back, we are trying to track down his killer that's all." James said soothingly.

"Okay then how can I help you ranger?" he asked.

"First tell me what you remember most about Jake?" Emmet sat for a moment in silence before he spoke.

"Jake like I said was a good man, he wanted to be a deputy here in Paris however his uncle talked him out of it that so he took a job as a guard riding shotgun on the Stage east to west across Texas. Most likely, with our low crime rate here, he would not have been shot dead."

"So do you think his uncle Jake is taking that pretty hard?"

"Wouldn't you?" Emmet responded.

"I suppose so, what else is there you can tell me about him?"

"Jake was a smart man, something had to happen that allowed another man to ride up behind them and shoot him and the driver. He was too careful would have never let someone sneak up on him!"

"Maybe he could not hear him riding up from behind while sitting over six galloping horses in front of him?"

"That is what I was trying to say, he would have been watching for someone coming at them from the rear!"

James thought for a moment then, excused himself letting Emmet return to his card game.

Ed asked, "What did you learn from Emmet if anything?"

"Nothing much he only remarked that Jake was a good man." James replied.

"So he had nothing really to add to what we already knew." Ed asked.

Just then, Sheriff Bailey pointed out Jake Roberts entering through the open doorway.
James said, "Edward, I'll let you talk to the Uncle about his nephew." Edward waited until Sheriff Bailey introduced him and asked if they could get a seat at one of the tables and talk.

They took the same table McCloud and Emmet had just left. "Mr. Roberts, I am here to ask a few questions about your nephew's death in the stage robbery six months ago? Is there anything you can tell me about young Jake?" asked Edward.

"What about it he was murdered, shot in the back by the stage robber, nothing more!"

"Could he have known who the robber was?" Ed questioned Jake.

"What are you saying you think he was in on it?"

"I did not say that I just asked if he could have known the man!"

"Hell No!" Mr. Roberts yelled. "You are making my nephew sound like he was in on the robbery and was murdered in the process. That is Bullshit and you know it!" Jake Roberts flipped the table over as he stood and drove his fist into Pinkerton's jaw knocking him across the room.

Sheriff Bailey and McCloud intervened before Roberts reached Ed to finish him.

"Jake, that's enough they are only trying to investigate young Jakes murder?"

"This little Bastard insulted my nephew and me, insinuating that Jake was in on the robbery and was shot because he knew who the robber was?"

McCloud helped Ed Pinkerton to his feet and checked his jaw. "You will have a nice bruise and it will be sore for a few days, but it is not broken. That's the good news!"

"You say that like there is bad news too!" Ed replied.

"There sorta is, you are not going to be chewing on anything like steak for awhile. By the way here is one of your molars I picked up off the floor."

McCloud and Bailey had them apologizing to each other after a few minutes of talking to each of the separately. Pinkerton spat blood into one of the spittoons along the brass foot rail running the length of the bar, tucking his tooth into his vest pocket.

Tom Bailey ordered up a bottle of whiskey they all sat down at the table they righted up on its pedestal.

Pinkerton grabbed one of the spittoons and brought it with him to the table. Hours later, they had cleared up what Ed Pinkerton was trying to find out about young Jake. Tom Bailey had mentioned that if Jake had known the man it would have made no difference in his murder, but he was positive that he would not have had part in the robbery or its planning. "Hell he wanted to be one of my deputies here."

Ed Pinkerton excused himself to head to the boarding house to see if he could get anything to put on his jaw.

McCloud asked. "How do you know so much about what happened on the stage that day?"
"I had went to retrieve Jakes body. I was there when the Marshal was interviewing the witnesses. Mrs. Denton she was the one he talked to the most"

"Mr. Roberts let me ask you in a different way that won't get my jaw busted. If young Jake had recognized the man who was going to rob them by remembering his face from a wanted poster. Would he had confronted him first and possibly called him by name?"

"No from what I understand from the woman whose husband was also murdered. She stated that she recognized him when she was shown some wanted posters of men with facial scars," He continued, "another passenger said he had heard Jake call the man Burl, but that could not have been possible as everyone else on the stage said that the driver and Jake were shot in the back from a distance. He then rode up on them and stopped the stage."

Tom Bailey said, "The newspaper story about the robbery stated the man later said he was not so sure about hearing Jake say anything before or after he was shot, he had just fallen from the seat and he was sure Jake was dead when he hit the ground."

"Was there any other information about the robbery, anything even if you do not think it was important?" James asked.

"Yeah there was one thing the lady said, that I thought was a bit strange."

"Strange, how?"

"She said that the robber right before he killed her husband, had called him by his name Michael, how would he had known her husband's name. They had never met before!"

"Were the couple on the stage going to someplace or returning home?" James asked him.

"She said they were traveling to visit a family member in Wichita Falls, they had boarded the stage in Lubbock and it was stopped about two hours from Wichita."

"Okay thank you Jake!"

McCloud passed on his condolences to Jake Roberts for Edward Pinkerton and himself.

By the next morning, Ed came down to breakfast and looked over at James sitting at a table alone. He walked over and joined him.

"Looks like you painted a fake beard on your chin it is so black!" James said.

Ed just pointed at his face and mumbled something James could not understand.

"Are you trying to tell me we are going to be riding quietly for a day or two?" asked James.

Ed just nodded, as the young lady came over to the table to take their orders.

"Let me order this time Ed, I'll have a skillet steak, eggs and fried potatoes. My friend here will have some coffee and Grits but make them real soupy he had an accident last night."

"Oh my Gawd, I would certainly say he had a pretty good accident. It hurts me just looking at his chin!"

After breakfast, James stated that they would be headed to Wichita Falls next.

"Why Wichita Falls he was last seen near Lubbock?" Pinkerton quizzed McCloud.

"You brought me along to do the tracking and that is what we are doing, so that is where we are headed next!"

The arrived in Wichita Falls, by noon and stopped by the Marshal's office. After introductions, James asked if he knew of any one with the last name Denton living nearby.

"Yes, there is a Mark Denton who works at the livery stables down the road two blocks at the saloon then North on Second Street, his brother was killed in a stage coach robbery a few months back?"

"Has he lived here long or is he a newcomer to town?" asked James.

"He and his brother grew up here, Michael married a young woman from Lubbock and they moved there right after the wedding." They thanked the Marshal and headed to the livery stables.

The large corral and barn was at the edge of town. The sign above the stable doors was worn painted wooden sign reading Penndel Livery Stables. They rode up to the hitching rail dismounted and wandered inside. Buzz Penndel was working at the anvil hammering a band for a barrel he was making for a customer. He looked up a welcomed his guests. "How can I help you Gents?" asked Penndel.

"I am Edward Pinkerton of the Pinkerton Detective Agency and this is James McCloud Texas Ranger we are here to ask a few questions if you have the time sir?"

"I am Buzz Penndel, Proprietor. What type of questions do you have?"

McCloud began, "Sir we have been looking for a man named Mark Denton who you might know, it has been said that he works here for you?"

"Mark quit work a week after his brother was murdered in a robbery. His brother and wife was on their way here by stagecoach when it has stopped and robbed of its strongbox and the passengers, three people were killed that day. Mark being the younger brother took it pretty darn hard. He grieved terribly and decided to go out in search of the robber and get his own kind of justice."

"Was Mr. Denton the type of guy whom could handle himself in a gunfight or up against another man in a fist fight?" asked Pinkerton.

"A fist fight for sure he held the bare knuckle boxing championship her in the county. As for a gunfight, he did carry a .50 caliper six-shooter and it was usually strapped down on his right side."

"Can you describe Mr. Denton to us, Mr. Penndel?" quizzed Pinkerton.

"Mark is about the same size as Ranger McCloud and has short grey balding head and a thick moustache that grows down to the bottom of his chin, and his chin is shaved clean as is the sides of his face," stated Penndel. Using his fingers to demonstrate the moustache by placing his two forefinger under his nose draws the across his upper lip and rounding his mouth down to his bottom chin line.

"Okay one last question did he indicate in anyway that he might know who he is looking for?" Pinkerton asked.

"He only had a copy of the wanted poster drawn and written description of the man he was looking for, however I had this feeling that he knew exactly who this man was?"

"How's that, what gave you that feeling he knew the robber? Had he indicated someway he knew of him." Asked McCloud.

"The day he left town he was ranting about getting revenge down at the saloon and was overheard by several men including the bartender. He had let it slip that he had fought a fist fight against Carlington a year ago and had beat him pretty bad, bad enough that he had broken the man's nose and had caused the cut on his face that had left the scar, everyone has described about Carlington."

"So he may not have known him personally?" Pinkerton declared.

"That has been the talk of the town since he left, di he or didn't he know the robber." Penndel said.

Edward thanked Mr. Penndel and he went back to hammering away at the band on the anvil.

"What do you think James, did he know Carlington and that is how Carlington knew Michael Denton's name?"

"Why don't we head down to the saloon and see what the town folk are saying and what if any of it is true!" replied McCloud.

They left their horses at the livery and walked back to the saloon.

They were still walking along Second street when the passed two local women of the town. Edward stopped tipping his Bowler styled hat asking them if he may query them with a question to two, holding the hard felt brown hat with a rounded crown against his chest. The ladies agreed and Edward asked if the knew Mr. Mark Denton a former livery stables worker? They said that they were very aware of the man as he has been the talk of the town since his departure months ago.

The lady dressed in the light blue blouse and long black wide pleated skirt with a large bustle that rode high in back, explained. "Mark is a handsome man in his mid-thirties and as far as we know he had never married!"

"That is nice to know ma'am but we are wanting to know more about his character, what type of man is he?" probed Edward. James leaned back against the wall of the department store propping one boot up against the wall he tipped the brim of his hat down blocking the afternoon sun from his eyes.

The second woman looked to be a little older than the first and closer to Mark's age stated.

"I was courted by Mark last year and he began our courting with kindness and attention to me. However, after a few weeks he became demanding and very jealous of me, especially if I spoke to another man!" she declared.

"Well as pretty as you are Ma'am, I would understand his jealousy, as a normal reaction!" she blushed at the comment by Edward.

"What sort of demanding characteristics did he express if I may ask?"

"Oh my, that is getting quite personal now sir!"

"Pardon me Ma'am for not introducing myself first; my name is Edward Pinkerton a Detective. We are trying to determine if Mr. Denton had the qualities of a good or bad man?"

She huffed, and answered him by saying, "You Sir do not need to delve into my personal relationship with Mr.

Denton, Let's go Lucy we are finished here!"

Edward looked over at McCloud bewildered.

"Well what did you expect, stopping two of the obviously prominent women of town?"

"I thought that they would be most likely to be the ones we could trust in the answers they would provide us!"

"Well you have obviously received your answer as expected then?" McCloud stated.

They continued towards the saloon with Pinkerton trying to explain his theories on the Pinkerton agency Interrogation techniques.

As they enter the saloon, James said. "Well Ed if you are planning to interrogate the citizens of this town we will get know where fast!"

"Just how do you think if we do not ask the tough questions the right way, that we would expect to get truthful answers?"

"Follow my lead in here and learn one or two ways from me sir." James said.

James ordered two beers and wandered on down to the end of the bar. Edward followed him and the bartender slid the mugs down the polished wooden bar to them. James was leaning with his back to the bar and the heel of his boot on the brass foot rail scanning the patrons that had stopped in for a late afternoon drink or two.

"Is this how you get the answers you need just by watching them?" Edward questioned.

"Be patient my friend, I will get around to talking to a few of them soon enough."

On his third mug of beer, James wandered over to a few men playing cards at one of the tables. They had just broken it up for a short break so that everyone could stretch there legs and ease the numbness in their butts from sitting in the wooden chairs. James bumping into one of them excusing himself stepping around the burly man.

"Pardon me sir I was looking over to the other side of the room, I thought I had recognized an old acquaintance of mine Mark Denton."

"Are you a friend of that scallywag Denton?" he said gruffly.

"No not a friend, I said an acquaintance. The difference is he is like, you said a scallywag I thought I seen the bugger here. How is that you know of him Mr. ugh, sorry I am new to town actually just passing through here on my way to Lubbock. My name is James!"

"Nice to meet you James, my name is Clint I own the Hardware store just up the street on the corner of Second."

"Oh yes I saw that place Griever's Hardware and Grain Company. I used to work for my father in his hardware store, mighty hard work but satisfying." James answered.

"That it is, James. That Mr. Denton feller had always seemed to be a bit on the shady side. Town's folk all thought the same, he would quite often be sneaking around at night when most everyone else had closed up and gone home."

"Maybe he was a night worker somewhere?"

"No, Denton worked for Penndel during the day at the Livery stables he would make and install the shoes for most of the horses boarding there, so he should have been too tired to be out all night!"

"Well that surely does sound like the same man I know of, I think he used to ride with a troublemaker named Burk or Bart something like that!"

"Yeah same guy for sure he rode with an outlaw named Burl Carlington for several years before he came back here where he grew up. That is why no one trusted him much!"

"Well again it was nice bumping into you Clint at least I know that he is here in town, where do you think I might find Denton this time of day?" McCloud asked.

"Oh you won't find him in town anymore he rode out after his brother was murdered in a stage coach robbery a few months ago."

"Well maybe next time I am through here he will be back in town?" McCloud tipped his hat and returned to the bar.

"Did you find out anything from the big guy over there? The way you walked right into him I thought we were going to have to fight our way out of here!"

"Nope, Clint owns the hardware store so that opened the door for us to chat it up about Denton, I found out that he had rode with Burl Carlington for several years. Most likely so did his brother Michael."

"That would answer how Burl knew to call out Michael Denton by name, they had rode together. And the fact that Burl has been a wanted man for least ten years they most likely rode together as outlaws!" recalled Edward.

"Reckon so!" stated James.

"I can see how you worked to get the information you needed, but how did you know which one of the men to talk too?"

"I listened to them talk over the game, Jason was the skinny fellow most likely is the man who runs the telegraph office, by the way he is always tapping is right hand forefinger, the guy sitting to his left runs the Bakery on fourth street. Gordy was the one in the dark brown vest by the tan line on his forehead he always wore a hat low on his head. So I assumed he works the fields of a farm nearby." James gulped down some of his beer before continuing. Carl is the town's banker he does not get out much during the heat of the day, and when he does he does not stay out to long, as pale as his skin is. Leaving Clint the Hardware store owner."

"So you picked Clint because you know so much about hardware stores from your past?"

"Well sort of, but if any of the others would have been as easy to accidently bump into, I could have brought up conversation about Banking, farming, or even asking how the bakery business was in town. That gets your foot in their door so to speak and then they are more willing to offer up information to a perfect stranger. While talking with Clint he confirmed my suspicions about the others and their lines of work."

"Good advice, I may have to try that approach some time. However, with my small stature, I better watch which size of a man to bump into! But it looks as if we have gotten enough information about Denton but nothing on Carlington the man we are looking for?"

"I beg to differ, Denton we know was bitter about his brothers murder, and he was most likely murdered because Michael could have identified him."

"Well we had already knew that much? What we don't know is where he is?"

"Again I beg to differ on that too, Carl came back and sat down at the table and was hearing what Clint and I were discussing and he stated that he heard from Mark Denton that he knew where Burl usually hides out. That he was headed there to confront Burl on the murder of his brother. Since he has not yet returned he has either not caught up to him yet or got himself killed by Burl in a gunfight!"

"So where is this hiding place?" asked Ed.

"That is going to be our next stop on the search, let's get the horses free from the luxury they have had all afternoon and I'll explain more as we ride along.

CHAPTER 3

They rode on along the trail meandering through the hills and valleys admiring the pristine beauty of the northeast Texas range. The sky was a bright blue with very little cloud cover and the temperature rose dramatically.

Argo feeling the discomfort of the sun, raised his head and nodded it, then casually walked off of the trail towards a stand of tall pines in search of shade.

Edward thought that James had planned to stop but wondered why he had not mentioned it before pulling out off the trail. "Heading for some shade, James I thought you were a hard man and could handle the sun's heat?"

"That I am but Argo here and a different idea on his own. He wanted a break in the shade so he decided to take a break and saunter over to the pines."

"You allow your horse to make your decisions for you?"

"He is not just my Horse and means of transportation but my Partner. If you cannot appreciate your partner's wishes then he no longer wants to appreciate you! Besides don't tell me you would not want to get out of the sun for a few minutes anyway partner?"

"You have a point there I would like to stretch my legs anyway." Replied Ed.

The trees proved beneficial as the temp seemed to drop several degrees as the ducked under the branches and moved further into the pines before stopping in an open area of prairie grass. James dismounted and removed the bridle from Argo before patting him on the neck. Argo stepped out into the shaded field and began chewing up some grass.

"You are not going to hobble him, what if he runs off? I have had many a horse simply dart away after they stepped into a spider web, or other unknown distractions."

"Like I said Argo is my partner and we rely on each other for survival, he will not be to far away at any point in time. We have an agreement I will take care of him and protect him with my life and he would do the same for me!"

Edward dismounted and led his horse out into the open grass. He removed the bridle from his horse. The young stallion sauntered out a few feet and turned his head back towards Edward. "Go ahead, I will be right here and I am trusting you to be on good behavior and stay close at hand?"

James cackled, "Well at least you asked him to stick around, maybe he heard you and understood."

"I am just trying to follow your lead." He remarked and laughed at himself.

James and Ed walked around for a few minutes to get the blood flowing into their legs before settling in and sat down leaning back on the trees.

Edward had swallowed a big gulp of water from his canteen and asked, "You suspect that Carlton is held up in that blind canyon?

"Yep, I remember that canyon from a few years back I used it to wait out a gang of bank robbers that favored that same canyon. Had the drop on them from the ridge, singlehandedly captured four and killed two, from that vantage point."

"What makes you think Carlton would not use the same tactics on us riding in?"

"I plan on him doing just that, he will hear us approaching as the sound of the hooves will bounce off the walls reaching the back where he will be camped way before we get we actually get Forty yards in!"

"Okay, so we are going into a positively unfeasible trap?"

"Nothing is a trap if you plan ahead for it?"

"Just how do you plan to sneak in, on foot?"

"No, that would not work either there is a flock of Sparrow like birds called the Towhee that are scattered about in the canyon. Each time you pass any of these little fellows hiding in the scrub they send out a warning call to the others it sort of sounds like *chili-chili-chili* and it is repeated in six to eight calls."

"Still tells me it is unachievable to get in there without getting killed. It is not likely we could just wait for him to come out to us that, could take days."

"Waiting for anybody is not in my playbook?" replied James.

Edward sat quietly for about ten minutes, before he asked again, "So what is in your playbook Ranger?"

"Like I said earlier Argo and I are partners and would lay down our live for each other if it comes to that?"

"You are going to send your horse in ahead of us as a decoy and chance getting him killed! That's crazy!"

"Yes it is but that is not the whole story. Argo is going to wander in as a lone stallion searching for mares, or a hiding area. Stirring up the birds and making enough noise that Carlton will get into position. If he takes up the best position available that is where we will capture him."

Edward still had a bewildered look on his face he again

sat quietly waiting for McCloud to drop the other shoe so to speak.

James did not make him wait long, "Edward here is where I test your mettle?"

"My What?

"Your courage, bravery, your determination?"

"I have plenty of courage, but I do not have a death wish!" Edward stammered.

"Good, then it is on as planned!" James replied confidently.

"As planned, are you going to share that plan with me anytime soon?"

James cleared an area of pine needles exposing the dirt below. He pulled a branch loose and cut a small section from it with his boot knife. With the small stick, he drew the canyon ridges and sides forming a long Vee in the dirt.

Edward spoke up "Okay so this represents the canyon?"

"No, it represents Geese flying north, as you can see this one line is longer than the other just like when you spot them in the sky. So do you know why one line is always longer than the other one?"

"No, why?"

"There are more birds in that line!" James cackled at his joke.

"I think you were out in that sun too long McCloud?"

"Actually, you were correct this does represent the canyon. His camp should be right about here." he marked a small X on the dirt near the closed end of the Vee, and continued. "The three best locations for his ambush are here, here and here." he said pointing them out with the stick. Two were on the East Ridge and one on the West.

"Which one did you use?" Edward asked.

"This one here, but he will not pick that one!"

"Why is that?"

"It was early morning when I last used the canyon and we are moving into late afternoon so he his going to want to have the sun to his back and the targets in the sunlight." So he will be over here," he said pointing at the East Ridge with the stick.

"What if he not alone in there, Denton did ride out here to confront him?"

"He may not be alone, but if Denton rode out here it wasn't to rejoin him, it was to kill him. So most likely he rode into the same ambush we are going to avoid."

James continued to draw out patterns with the stick and answer questions from Edward. James kicked the dirt around scuffing up the drawing and said, "Well it is getting to be about the right time to move out. Let's saddle up?"

They rode on for another hour until the canyon came within sight from the trail.

"This is where we part, you take that trail there and follow the plan we discussed. I will wait out here until I think you are in place, so don't dally around!"

"I won't you can count on that!" Edward remarked.

James dismounted and removed Argo's saddle and bridle. He brushed him down of the heavy sweat where the saddle had been and had Argo lay down on the trail. With a couple of hand motions Argo rolled around onto his back and moved around like he was trying to reach an itch in the middle, then jumped back up on his feet. James was now satisfied that Argo looked more like a wild stallion as the walked on ahead to the opening to the canyon. As they entered into the canyon, James waited until they were in roughly fifty yards. He stepped in front of Argo, "I know that you really do not understand everything I say however I am gonna say it anyway. I need you to mosey on into this canyon as if you were looking for a couple young mares to visit with. I know you would like that, if they would happen to be in there! We are after a wanted killer so I would advise you not to get yourself killed or shot. So get along now and give me the distraction I need to get in there behind you and capture that critter.

Agro simply trotted off into the canyon as if he heard and understood every word spoken.

"Damned if he ain't doing exactly what I asked, as long as he moves all the way into the canyon far enough?"

Edward had rode around the East Ridge and tied off his horse to a brush stand, he started his long hard climb up the back of the canyon plateau. He stopped just long enough to get a rock out of his boot and gulped down some of his water; he spilled a little on his handkerchief and wiped his face and balding head. Moving on over the edge of the canyon watching his footing carefully to be sure, he did not tumble or loosen any of the stones giving away his position. Checking his pocket watch he had taken just over fifty-five minutes to get into position that James marked, even though he was not totally positive it was the exact spot he had marked he estimated he was as close as he wanted to be to Burl Carlton.

Burl had heard Argo entering the canyon, he moved along the lower edge of the West Ridge staying in the shadows of the sun's shade. Darting across the canyon, he climbed up the east side cliffs to a small landing with a wind driven cave cut into its side. It was a perfect position for an ambush on the unsuspected incoming rider.

McCloud was maneuvering into position along the west wall keeping under the shade he moved slowly and carefully, keeping out of sight. He found a good hiding position just yards down from the bend in the canyon beyond that Burl would have him in his sights even while hiding in the shade.

Burl caught site of the lone stallion entering the canyon and relaxed, placing his rifle against the large boulder he was behind for cover. "A wild horse, I should have just shot the damn thing. But no use killing a good horse, Hell I might even try to capture it and have fun trying to break him into a riding pony." He said to Denton.

Denton had tried sneaking into the canyon just a couple weeks ago. He was shot as he dropped over the ledge landing right where Carlton was now standing.

"I thought we had another visitor Mark, but it is just another wild horse looking for mares or water?"

From just above and to the south just yards away from Edward he heard him speaking to Denton, totally surprised that Mark had joined up with him after he had killed his only brother! He could easily see Carlton but Denton had to be further back closer to the wall, hidden from view.

"Carlton I have the drop on you if you move an inch I will fire this rifle blowing your ass off the ridge?"

"Who is up there? If you have me in your sights I should be able to see the man who is about to shoot me. Step on out in the open and look me in the face, before you kill me?"

Burl knew he was fast with his Colt .44 and should be able to get a shot off before the bounty hunter could fire his rifle while he was moving to stand and show himself.

Edward instead tossed his Bowler hat over the boulder

he was behind keeping his rifle sights trained on Burl's chest.

McCloud was listening opposite of them across the narrowest section of the canyon. He slowly moved further in until he could see Carlton's back, his waist just below and behind the large boulder above.

"Burl Carlton, I am Edward Pinkerton, Detective and I was hired by the Overland Stage Coach Company to bring you in to stand trial?"

Burl yelled out, "I am not going anywhere and there is no way you can get to me from up there, so you either show yourself and die quickly or you back out of there your decision?"

"Burl, you know I cannot do that the Pinkerton Agency signed a contract to bring you in. Dead or Alive, that is your decision." Ed yelled back at him. He was now wondering if all this bantering back and forth was just allowing Denton to move around and getting in behind him. In addition, he did not know if McCloud had made it into the canyon. His mind began whirling, *What if he had been bitten by a Rattlesnake or was held back by another member of the gang.' Hell, McCloud said himself, he did not know if he was alone or with a group of men, holed up in the box canyon.* Panic was now settling in on the portly detective.

James had removed his belt buckle, the backside of it was highly polished and he used it to reflect a few flashes from the sun, up above Carlton. Ed was crouched down low now and did not see any of them, however Burl caught sight of the light bouncing off of the rocks. Quickly dropping to his knees behind the boulder, grabbing ahold of the Winchester rifle. Carlton laid down and scanned the ever-growing darkness of the far side of the canyon looking for who was down there signaling the Detective.

He caught the last few flashes locating the other bounty hunter.

McCloud had noticed that Burl had quickly ducked down. James also dropped for cover just as he heard the Crack echoing in the canyon. The shot hitting him on his left shoulder. The bullet had torn through his outer sleeve; blood was now running down dripping from his fingertips. James ripped at his shirtsleeve seeing that the bullet passed clean through the large muscled shoulder. He moved his arm slowly feeling the pain and smelling the burn flesh, he was certain that it had missed the bone.

"Damnit, he said to himself that was a stupid mistake, I should have gotten under cover first?" He ripped the rest of his sleeve away and tied it around his upper arm to slow the bleeding.

Hearing the exchange of rifle fire Edward popped his head up just enough to see Burl sprawled out on the ledge firing down on McCloud. He rested his Henry rifle on the boulder and shot two rounds into Carlton's back the dark maroon blood was quickly pooling around his body and running over the ledge.

McCloud heard the distinct rifle shots from the Henry and yelled up to Pinkerton.

"Ed, was that you doing the shooting just now?"

"Yeah, I got Carlton in the back, but I think Denton is up here somewhere. I heard Burl talking to him?" Ed yelled down to McCloud.

Both men held their cover for another ten minutes without hearing anything moving around them or anywhere in the canyon. Moments later Argo came walking back to where James was crouched down.

James noticed that Argo was not indicating any other dangers nearby as he just munched on the leaves of the bushes at the canyon ridgeline. Again, he thought, *"If, Argo feared that someone else was close by he would have stayed back under cover himself?"* James called out to Pinkerton, "No one else is left in here but the two of us, I have a minor bullet wound in my left shoulder. If you have not been shot, can you work your way down from there?"

"On my way now, but I did hear Burl clearly talking to Denton, he even called him by name?"

"I'll keep you covered from here as you work your way down, and be aware of any Rattlers in those rocks?"

Ed helped bandage McCloud's arm properly, both had agreed that the bullet had missed hitting any bones and had passed through only the shoulder muscle. They moved further into the canyon heading to where Carlton had made camp. Within fifty yards of where James was shot, they found the bloated and decaying body of Mark Denton. James had pointed out that he was most likely dead for at least a week or more.

While James walked Argo out to get his saddle. Edward took the canvas Carlton had used for a lean-to tent and climbed back up to his dead body, wrapping it up to bring it down to the valley floor.

When Ed made it back down with Carlton's body, they piled rocks on the two bodies for burial, being no other way to dig a hole in the rock canyon floor.

James and Edward rode together on Argo, around the canyon to where Pinkerton had tied off his horse. Heading back for Dallas.

When they finally arrived, and were standing at the double doors to the Regional Office McCloud paused pointing out the new sign.

"TEXAS RANGERS" and Texas Ranger Star, two feet in diameter. Just below the Star was the words Regional

Office, Dallas Texas, and Captain – Terrance Vance, Commander Texas Rangers. They entered and James introduced Edward Pinkerton to Captain Vance and explained how the mission had been completed with Pinkerton killing Carlton and that Burl Carlton had also murdered Mark Denton, the older brother to Michael Denton killed in the Overland Stage robbery.

Pinkerton announced the case closed and headed for the Telegraph office to inform the Pinkerton Agency.

James stopped by the Doctor's office and had his wounds properly cleaned and stitched up. Taking a few days off to recover fully.

CHAPTER 4

Dallas Regional Office, Texas Rangers
Two weeks later;

James McCloud, Texas Ranger cinched up his gun belt and putting on his rider's vest with the Gold Ranger Star over the left side as he was headed for the door of the Texas Rangers regional office.

Captain Vance yelled out to him. "McCloud we all know you like to work alone and we all understand and appreciate that. However, this time we may need you to go to see Marshal Bode Johnson in Steele Creek, Texas."

"What kind of problem is he having down there?" he asked from the doorway.

"Come on back to my office we need to talk?"

McCloud pulled the door closed and followed Vance to his office.

Sitting in his office in Dallas, Terrance Vance begins to tell a story of a small South Texas town and its history to Ranger James McCloud.

"The beginning story"

Texas, 1887, a tiny incidental desert hamlet named Steele Creek. A little known, seldom spoken southern town nestled beneath majestic mountains along the southwestern border between Texas and Mexico, and morally hovering between virtue and corruption. It is commonplace community barely on the maps of this vast region, a unique shade of gray in this harsh black and white world. It is a tiny culture unto itself where the splendid sometimes means the surreal. It is a place where wandering souls come for a variety of reasons. For some it is to seek a better life away from the increasingly modernized mayhem of progress, it is a sanctuary from the past, a transcendent place of sorts to start once again.

The town of Steele Creek is many things to many people, for the residents merely a place where they try to live their lives according to their wants and beliefs. Each man, woman and child who stops there knows and understands that every day is another precious opportunity to fulfill a dream, to realize happiness or to achieve redemption. For those souls who wander there searching for comfort, retribution or a just brief, sanctuary from their sobering lives, they'll find their journey's end has led the to a point of decision. A decision everyone must make upon arrival at Steele Creek.

A town where Cowmen meet new beginnings, a town on the edge of the American spirit, where the unimaginable is cultivated from the seeds of the human condition. Steele Creek a town where the past and the present roll the dice with the future hanging in the balance."

Continuing the story Terrance Vance introduces Bode Johnson's history to James.

"Throughout his life he must face many forms of misfortune whether it be his life style, his beliefs and fears or even his own mortality. It is what a man chooses to do when those moments arrive that determines the character and tenacity of a man. Some may choose to ignore the situation while others may turn away in abject terror of the significances and after-effects. Still others will act with bravado in the absence of any other believable alternative.

As a forty-three year old man of good health and sound mind trying to find his way through an unforgiving land with a moral compass that is less than true. Bode is seeking what most of us want in our short time on this earth, a chance to live a normal life with normal cares and normal circumstances. His journey to this point has being anything but normal however. It has been a life of self-indulgence laden with a stunted conscience and a vague code of ethics. However, he is rapidly approaching a fork in the road of his destiny and he will have to make a very significant decision. It is a decision, which will demand a lifetime commitment.
However, one very important detail may have a heavy bearing on his selection.
You see Bode Johnson had a secret."

McCloud steadfast quietly listens to Vance's story

"Although quiet and unassuming on his surface, he is not a man to be philandered with. He is what people in this land call a gunfighter, a hired gun, a shootist. He is a man who prefers to settle his confrontations with the absolute finality of his revolver rather than civil discourse. By all accounts, he is a cold-blooded killer whose weapon of choice is the unforgiving bullet from a Colt .45. It has been said that he has no soul and that when he dies even The Devil himself will not let him into Hell."

"Bode driven to present legend by the deadly success of his past. It is a past compiled from bullets and blood, guns and graves. It is a life of self-indulgence through intimidation and fear, of fame and fortune at the barrel of a gun. However, that reputation has outgrown its usefulness and its appeal. It has become a burdensome life of running from town to town, keeping three steps ahead of the law and the hangman to avoid paying the final bill on his troubled history. That escape has brought this man to his current quandary."

McCloud nods his head confirming Vance's description as Terrance continued.

"The tragic truth is he is a tired man now. He has grown weary of living off his gun. Death is a repulsive notion for him these days. He knows it could come the next time his gun swings from his holster. He would like to stop running, settle down and live out the rest of his life in peaceful inscrutability.
His pursuit of that end has unknowingly led him there to a deadly penance and this time his lethal prowess with a six-gun may not put the odds in his favor. The man's dark past had caught up with him. He will have to confront that dark past just as we all must on the day of our final judgment at a location yet to be determined. As this man, his judgment day of life will most definitely transpire there at Steele Creek."

CHAPTER 5

Captain Terrance Vance at the Texas Ranger Regional Office Dallas, Texas finished the story of Steele Creek and about the Outlaw Bode Johnson, and his 'Wanted Poster' hanging in the front window of the Regional Texas Rangers Office.

McCloud is fascinated by the story, but is not convinced that any outlaw so cruel and destructive to life could change himself.

Captain Vance speaks up again,
"The Texas Governor has granted Johnson his pardon from his crimes to date. I agreed to honor that with a stipulation that we confirm that he has indeed turned his life around in peaceful anonymity. And that will be your undertaking." Vance explains.

Terrance removed the wanted poster and marked it as a 'Closed Case' asking McCloud to ride south and provide any assistance he could muster for Bode.
McCloud agreed to ride down into southern Texas and meet this 'Former Outlaw' now the infamous Marshal, to see what he can do to help the newly elected Marshal of Steele Creek, or bring him back to face his past.

McCloud stepped out the big double doors a walked down the steps thinking to himself; well I sure hope that they this Outlaw has truly changed and is now who his story claims him to be!

James McCloud, Texas Ranger cinched up his gun belt and putting on his rider's vest with the Gold Ranger Star over the left side, he was headed for the door where outside waiting for him was his horse Argo quietly waiting in the shade near the water trough.

Argo a stallion with great markings of the white flecks on chestnut coat and white full-face blaze, and carried black larger spots on his quarters. McCloud cherished the horse as he had carried him though most of Texas and beyond. Argo was more to him then a simple mode of transportation, as they over time became inseparable partners, each learning and teaching the rules and dangers that the New Territory presented.

James always stated that Argo was just as much a Texas Ranger as he was Loyal, Honest, and full of Integrity.

Reaching into his saddle bag he removes a wax paper wrapping of brown molasses and oats mixed into apple sized clumps and feeds a few to Argo, brushing his hand up Argo's face from his soft nose to between his ears, stopping there to scratch his head.

Argo returns the affection by first rubbing his forehead on McCloud's chest. Then abruptly raising his head knocking James off his feet. James landed on his Ass and rolled into a somersault kicking his feet over his head returning to a standing position facing Argo.

Argo took a few steps back wards, crossed his front legs and bowed to James.

"Good one old man, so you think that was funny?" James stepped forward as Argo returned to his upright stance nodding his head up and down as if saying, yes!

"Well I hope you got that out of your system for now, we have some miles to cover. Argo stepped up and rubbed his nose on McCloud's cheek. "Okay enough of that flirting with me, here have a few more of these oat and molasses' balls."

James mounted the saddle and they trotted out of town.

CHAPTER 6

"New Life, May 1886"

Bode Johnson felt very weary as he rode his appaloosa along the dusty street, past the people as they walked along the boardwalk. As he sauntered down the street, he could feel a difference about this town. Not in the weight of their stares. For the first time in a long time, he did not know what they were thinking. He could almost smell a change in the dusty air.

They were not afraid of him. It did not matter who he was. He felt a grousing in his stomach as he pushed his dusty hat down in back up off his brow, wiping his forehead of gritty sweat. He was very tired after the six months of jumping from town to town across the southwest, then another long ride from the tiny border town of San Verde where he had spent the last several months. It had been a peaceful town, much smaller compared to the one. He would have liked to stay there but a little disagreement with a local lawman that had hastened the necessity of his departure.

'Why didn't he walk away? He thought. 'No, he couldn't just walk away from her. That would look bad for such a macho hombre like him. The damned fool! He shivered as if a cold chill went through his soul.

The damned stupid fool!" he said aloud, his teeth clenched. He coughed hard, his throat dry from the trail dust. His eyes slowly surveyed the street for the town's saloon.

Every town has a saloon just as every town has a lawman and a doctor, two things that he has seen too much of in his lifetime. Yes sir, every town surely is the same in every town he thinks 'maybe this time it'll work. Maybe this time I'll be able to put an end to it all'. However, in all the previous towns, despite his optimism, he had only lying to himself. He had been proven wrong so many times. Nevertheless, there seems to be something different here, in this town, something that gave him a glimmer of hope.

He rode up in the front of the primary drinking enterprise Greyson's Forty Rivers Saloon. He glances up at the huge, weatherworn painted wooden sign and chuckles to himself.

"Forty Rivers, cold beer and warm women" huh? Guess that is fitting, he thinks with a grin.

He dismounts and ties the reins to the hitching post. Stepping onto the boardwalk, he walks through the batwing doors into the saloon. Once inside pausing there, scouring the scene for anything that might disrupt his intentions. Usually that disruption came with a badge. Satisfied with the layout's regulars, he makes his way to the far end of the bar, here he could watch his back as there would be nothing but a wall behind him.

"Yes sir?" said the barkeep.

"Bottle of your best whiskey," he said quickly.

"No problem as I always serve my best" replies the somnolent bartender as he recedes to the far end of the bar. He returns a few seconds later with a bottle and pulls the cork before sliding it gently to the waiting man, setting a shot glass on the bar top. Bode fills the glass and downs it. Pouring himself a second shot, he speaks.

"You Greyson?" he asked the barkeep without taking

his eyes off his shot glass.

"Yes sir, Hank Greyson, proprietor", he replied. "And you Mister?

"Johnson, Bode Johnson", Johnson smiles as he downs the glass once again "Any hints as to where can I might get a nice quiet room?"

"Well there's Miss Veolia's Boarding House down the street or the Brazos Hotel just beyond that. Both have good rooms for a fair price"

"Much appreciative," said Johnson slapping a bright silver dollar onto the bar. It was sure that it was more than the liquor cost but Bode felt that he might as well set about to creating good will between himself and the town.

"Thank you!" Greyson shouted as Johnson disappeared through the front doors. "Come again, sir, come again indeed!"

Bode paused on the boardwalk, looking up and down the bustling street. He smiled and began walking up the street. For the first time in a very long time, his heart felt light as if a heavy dark weight had been removed. He tipped his hat to an extravagantly dressed young woman. She smiled shyly as she passed him. There was no trembling at his face, no cowering at his presence. There was no cursing his name to the Devil below, all things, which had previously been daily occurrences in his life.

"Whoa..!" he said with a surprise as someone carrying two full bags of groceries came bounding out the door of Red River's Dry Goods and run straight into him. All the content of the bags spilled to the ground and scatter along the boardwalk.

I'm so sorry!" came a voice as light and sweet as fresh spun honey. Bode turned his gaze from the fallen groceries up to a lovely face. His eyes met hers and his heart nearly leapt from his chest. Standing there was a woman dressed in a flannel checked shirt and jeans. She was a beautiful woman, maybe about thirty, with lightly reddish hair that fell down around her face in ringlets. Her face was thin with high cheekbones. She wore no make-up not all fancied up as many of the women about town were. No, she had a natural beauty to her. Her figure was slender but one could tell she was not frail by any means, she looked strong and yet petite. However, the thing he noticed most about her was her eyes. It was not so much the color he was struck by an emerald green but more what he saw in her eyes. They were bright and caring but there was more to them than that. It was as if there was an emptiness hidden amidst the sparkle, almost as if they were longing for something or perhaps someone.

"I am very sorry, sir!" her troubled voice snapped him back to the moment. "I wasn't paying attention I guess and. . ."

"Oh my please, please I should've been more careful. Here let me help." He said never taking his eyes from her face.

They quickly gathered up her things and had them securely back in their bags. They both reached for the last remaining item on the boardwalk, a shiny red apple, one of many she had bought their hands touched for a second. There was an awkward silence of embarrassment and then Bode withdrew his hand. She picked up the apple and placed it gently into one of her bags.

"Well thank you very much Mister... uh?" she inquired.

Did he dare? Did he dare look her in the eye and risk the chance that his reputation may have already made it to this town? He drew a long breath. He could feel his heart begin to race. Although not so very noticeable, his usually steady hands began to tremble. Think hard, 'What was the name I just gave the bartender, ah yes Johnson one of many he had used over the years try to hide his identity.'

He swallowed hard, smiled and replied.
"Johnson. Bode Johnson." A nervous grin appeared as

he looked into her eyes. "And please, don't give it a second thought, Mrs. uh . . . ?"

"Mica O'Shea. Mica pronounced 'MyCAA,' Mica O'Shea." She answered with a smile.

"Mica, huh? That's Iri..." he searched for the words that would not make him appear as prejudice. He should have known that a woman such as her would already be spoken for. He tries to hide his disappointment as he continues, "that's a wonderful name. I have a niece named Mikala that lives back east we refer to her as Mikey" he lied.

"Why thank you, Mr. Johnson." She said, her eyes twinkling even brighter now. "Are you staying in town long?"

"I'm not sure exactly. It is a very fine town for sure. In addition, if the sights around the rest of the town are as nice as the ones I have seen so far, well… I just may stay around for awhile."

Mica could feel her cheeks flush as she blushed. Bode gave a half-chuckle at the sight

"Well maybe I'll see you around then, Mr. Johnson," she said adjusting the bags of groceries in her arms.

"Please, call me Bode." he said with a smile in his eye.

"Very well… Bode" she replies as she begins to walk away. "And by the way…"

Bode pauses from his admiring the swaying gate of her walk to hear her words.

"…It's Miss." She said, never turning back because she just knew he was watching. She smiled as she strides away. The smile broadens on Bode Johnson's face.

"Yes sir," he said under his breath, "I just might be here awhile at that!"

He nods his head subconsciously and continues down the street with a little bit more of a skip in his step.

Midmorning finds Bode Johnson seated alone at a table

in the Steele Point Diner located in the southern most part of the town. The pancakes are cold, the coffee bland and the eggs are tougher than boot leather but despite all of the distractions, he finds the meal one of the best he has had in a long time. In his line of work, he was used to eating beans and sand on a skillet out on some lonesome prairie or holed up by some campfire. He shudders as if to shake those memories from his head and shoves another piece of steak into his mouth. He just knew that things were going to be different here. He could feel it in his soul. This was the place where he would turn his life around. He just flat out knew it. However, he reminded himself that the change would not come overnight.

'One day at a time, old boy, one day at a time.' he smiled as the thought ran its course.

He absentmindedly glances out the window behind his table. Suddenly a smile appears on his face. He quickly stands up and taps vigorously on the window. He motions for the object of his attention to come inside. He stands awkwardly at his table waiting anxiously, wringing his hands together. Then in through the doors walks a smiling Mica O'Shea.

"Why Mr. Johnson, nice to see you again" she said in that smooth Texas drawl of hers.

Bode pulls out a second chair and offers it to her.

"Please, call me Bode" he said.

"Oh yes, right" she said, a childish smile appearing on her lips," Bode."

She sits down and Bode tucks her chair in to the table. He motions for a waiter to come.

"I know it may be a bit forward of me, just meeting you today and all, but would you do me the honor of having dinner with me tonight? I am new here and do not yet know anybody else in town and." he asks.

"Well. . . I appreciate the kind offer, I really do," she said,

"But. . . " adds Bode dolefully.
"I have a previous dinner engagement, I'm afraid."

The disappointment was very evident on Bode's face. 'Of course there has to be another man in her life, she is too nice looking to be alone. Besides why would this lovely woman want to spend time with a man like me' he thought to himself, quickly trying to mask the hurt with a simple smile but he was transparent in the attempt. Mica had already seen it.

"You see, I'm cooking for the church's bean supper tonight," she said.

"The... church?" said Bode as the smile slowly returned to his face.

"Yes, the Baptist, down at the end of First Street" she added.

"Really?" said Johnson with a titter in his voice.

I'd love to see you there" she replies.

"You just may at that, Mica"

"Well... good! I look forward to it then" she said, standing up from the table. "By the way, you like the food here?"

Johnson stands as well, tipping his hat as she sashays from the table.

"I've had a lot worse," he said with a smile.

'Well you'll have to stop by tomorrow for lunch," she said as she walks behind the counter. "You're looking at the newest head chef of this Diner." She winks.

Johnson watched as she disappeared through the swinging doors leading into the kitchen, Mica quickly glancing back at him as well.

"Yup," he said under his breath, "I sure do think I'm gonna like it here."

Bode sat back down to finished his breakfast with a steady grin on his face.

Days turned into weeks, weeks turned into months and

over that time, Bode relentlessly pursued Mica as a suitor. Eventually Mica consented to courting and the two became fast friends. Love blossomed between the two and Bode would wake up at night in disbelief at the good turn his life had taken.

CHAPTER 7

"Day of Reckoning September 1886"

Bode Johnson soon became a fixture in the average town. He'd come to have many friends and they learned to like and admire Bode Johnson for his character and smiling, gentle manner. Over this time, Bode Johnson went through a transformation in both conscience and character. He became a man who gained the respect and trust of all whose path he crossed. He was viewed as a firm but fair individual by those he worked with. He also gained the reputation of being dependable, easygoing and hardworking.

It had been a whirlwind of events since he had decided to stay here. He had gotten a good paying job as ranch foreman at the Two R's Ranch run by Randy Reeder.

He had barely settled into the job when his valor was put to the test by a gang of cattle rustlers. Eric Desmond, his brothers Theo, Brian and Darrell plus local gunman Brock Cody all plotted to rustle some of Randy Reeder's cattle as they grazed about in a grassy field a mile north of town.

It was early evening when Brian, Darrell and Cody sat in Patrick O' Grady's Saloon drinking and playing cards. A very drunk Brian began bragging about what they planned on doing the following night He was overheard by Ric Whalen, the saloon's bartender. Whalen, being good friends with Bode, went to him with the plot.

The next evening Johnson and fellow ranch hands Jimmie Nevin and Charlie McKay rode out to the pasture at dusk. They stayed along the tree line so as not to be readily seen as they waited. It was a full moon and it lit up the hillside with a soft silvery glow, enough to see anyone coming or going.

Their wait was rewarded quickly as just after dusk a group of riders slowly and quietly made their way down the crease of the valley where the cattle were grazing by a stream. Sure enough, it was the Desmond Brothers and Brock Cody cutting out some cattle as they grazed in a low valley. The trio rode up and confronted the group. Eric was not among them when the confrontation occurred. There was a standoff, as Johnson demanded that the rustlers leave or face the consequences. Just what those consequences were, nobody knew but Bode.

In his previous profession, he had become quite accustomed to reading people. It paid to know those you were up against and their character. Subtle things such as the way a man wore his holster or the way he may place his hands during a conversation all gave partaking of to what that man is thinking about doing. Johnson sized up each and every man. He knew the men on his side. Jimmie Nevin was an over-ambitious kid with a chip on his shoulder but a good sense of right and wrong. He would be quick on the draw but more than likely wild on his execution. Charlie McKay on the other hand was a salty veteran of range wars and knew how to handle himself and his gun in tight situations such as these. Bode knew they both had sand and would stand by him to the finish.

On the other side of the matter were the rustlers. Theo Desmond was a coward, plain and simple. He was a bull shitting hard talker but he would be the last to shoot and the first to run. His brother, Brian was the eldest of the clan. He had had a hard life and really was not itching to die but he was a steady hand with a six-shooter. He might listen to reason before any gunplay. Darrell Desmond was a follower. He would watch Brian or Theo to see their reactions and then jump onboard accordingly. Bode knew if he could talk Brian into just leaving then Darrell would not make a play on his own. The last of the bunch was the wildcard. Brock Cody.

Brock Cody was a big man, about six foot-three or four, with hair as black as night and eyes filled with bad purpose. Bode knew of Cody and his handiwork with a six-gun but even If he had not, he would know Brock was a hired gun, no doubt about it. He had the hat pulled down to hide his eyes and intentions. His holster was tied down to his leg, sure sign of someone who works forcefully with a pistol. He was calm and cool as if out for a Sunday ride. Not even a hint of nerves. That is the sign of a man harboring the silent confidence of his ability with a shooting iron. Yeah, Brock Cody was the one to watch for if the situation started going south.

"Brian! Listen Brian there ain't no need for this!" shouts Bode across the herd at Brian Desmond just a mere twenty-five feet away.

"We're takin' this herd" he spit back. "Eric had told McKay if you crossed our water again we'd take measures. You did not listen to Eric and now we are takin' 'em!"

"Not likely, Brian" said Bode. "These are Two R's cattle, Brian and you know we're running them up to the north pasture where they'll get branded. Why are you rustling them?"

"Hey, there ain't no brands on them right now. That's makes them fair game far as I can see." said Brian with a sly grin as looks at each of his compatriots.

Bode looked them over as well. Theo was nervous and had slowly moved to the back of the pack. Darrell was wide-eyed, looking at everyone, his left hand slowly making its way to his gun. Brian kept eye contact, he was talking and that was a good thing for the moment. It was Brock Cody however, who had Bode's full attention now Cody had shifted his weight in his saddle. He was now sitting upright, one hand with the reins resting on the saddle horn. Cody's other hand was rubbing his belt buckle as if he was polishing it with his glove, getting closer and closer to his pistol with each rub.

"Look Brian, you go now and this ends here. I give you my word," said Bode.

Brian's eyes wander to his friends then back to Johnson.

"Oh we're gonna leave here alright but the cattle's coming with us. Unless you plan on helping us, I would suggest you go back to the bunkhouse, drink some coffee. Forget we were ever here."

"I don't think he's gonna help us, Brian. I think maybe he is thinking' of trying' to stop us. Is that right, Mr. Foreman?" said Cody is a gruff voice. "You itching to play hero?"

Bode looked back at Brian. Brian is eyeing Johnson, trying to gauge Bode's reaction.

"C'mon Brian, this don't need to happen. Move on and we'll all live to see another day, huh?"

"They ain't going to leave unless we make 'em leave, Bode," whispers Jimmie.

"Easy Jimmie, let me handle this"

"What do you say, Brian? Is a few rustled head of cattle worth risking everybody getting killed?"

Bode glances over at Cody. His hand is almost on his pistol now.

The tension amongst the group was escalating and Bode knew he had to diffuse the situation quickly or risk an all out gunfight "Darrell, talk some sense to him will you," he said with a harsh tone.

"What's the play, Brian?" asked Darrell.

"He'll go straight to the law, Brian and you know it.

Let's finish this." Cody grumbled.

"Brian, don't do this," said Bode, his right hand slowly descending to his side.

"Just shut up!" Brian snaps. "I just want to. . . "

"You know what Eric said to do if we ran up against them. If you ain't got the sand to do this then let me," said Cody, slowly moving his horse to the side, putting some space between himself and the rest of the group.

Bode knows the play all too well. He also knows that now there will be no room for error. His right index finger was now absentmindedly tapping the handle of the pistol on his right hip.

"So, he speaks for you and your brothers now, huh Brian? All he's gonna do is get you killed."

"Who's gonna do the killing', greenhorn? You? I highly doubt it" Cody spits the words out as he draws his pistol. Bode was ready and flays his leather in one fluid motion. CRACK!
CRACK!

Two shots ring out. Cody's shot goes wide of Bode while Cody is hit in the shoulder and knocked from his horse by Bode's bullet. Seeing the firing commence, Jimmie Nevin draws his pistol and fires at Darrell and Brian, both shots missing them, as they attempted to scatter but pinned in place by the scampering herd. As they spin on their horses, Charlie McKay raises his rifle and fires a shot at Theo who is trying to ride away. Bode looks at Cody slumped on the ground and motionless. He quickly dismounts his horse seeking his footing.

CRACK!

A bullet whistles past Bode's ear. Instinctively he quickly turns and fires again.

CRACK!

Brian Desmond is hit in the belly. He raises his pistol and fires off a round that hits Charlie McKay in the left leg. Bode sees the injury and grits his teeth in anger. Then suddenly al emotion drains from his face. His angered expression is now replaced by a stoic stare. He calmly levels his pistol again.

CRACK!

This shot hits Brian Desmond in the chest instantly knocking him from his saddle to the ground. Darrell Desmond fires off a shot that knocks Jimmie Neven's hat from his head as he is reloading his gun. Bode calmly but quickly turns towards the fray and squeezes the trigger once more.

CRACK!

Darrell Desmond gun falls from his hand as he tumbles backwards off his horse and hits the ground with a thud.

CRACK!

Charlie McKay fires another shot at the fleeing Theo Desmond. Bode Johnson spins around to the direction of the rifle's report, his six-gun still gripped tightly in his hand. He squeezed the trigger with the gentleness of handling an egg.

CRACK!

Theo Desmond bows forward in the saddle, a result of Bode's bullet's impact to his back Theo Desmond then slumps to his right and falls from his saddle to the ground.

His blood pooled around his chest down the side, soaking into the san and then there was silence.

Light blue gun smoke fills the air as Bode sits in his saddle at the ready for further gunplay. He quickly eyes the tragic scene.

"Whose hit?" shouts Bode as he walks over to the side of the fallen Brian Desmond? Brian lay dead on the ground, his pistol still gripped in his left hand. Bode shook his head in disgust.

"Didn't need to go down like this, you damned fool," he said under his breath.

"I-I'm okay" stammers Jimmie as he pokes a finger through the hole in his hat.

Bode spins his horse around trying to find McKay.

"Charlie? Charlie?" he shouted.

"Over... here..." a familiar grizzled voice hollered. The cattle had scampered away and Bode could see McKay now. He had pulled himself up against a rock, his left leg bloodied just below the knee. Bode guided his horse to McKay's position and dismounted.

"Is it bad, Charlie?" asks Bode, quickly wrapping his neckerchief around the wound.

"Nah, I think it went clean through" said Charlie.

"Bode!" screams Jimmie.

Bode turns toward Jimmie's voice and sees the winged Cody standing there, pistol in his hand. The gunman levels his pistol at Bode.

"You're done, Johnson!" shouts Cody.

CRACK!

"Bode!" screams Jimmie as he turns his horse and races to his foreman's side. As he reaches the area, he stops his horse dead in his tracks as Bode spins around and trains his gun on him.

"Whoa, Bode, It's me!" said Jimmie, his eyes wide at the gruesome sight before him. Brock Cody lay dead on the ground, a second bullet wound to the forehead.

A smoking gun is held tightly in the right hand of Bode Johnson and is now pointed at Jimmie himself. He just stands there and stares down at Bode who is in a slightly crouching position beside the body of Cody.

"Easy Bode, it is all over, Bode?" said Jimmie.

Bode is motionless, staring wild-eyed at Jimmie as if still in the heat of the fight.

"Bode?" he said again as if trying to wake Johnson from his frenzied gaze. "Bode!" Jimmie is now sure Bode is going to shoot him too!

Johnson blinks a few times, as he appears to come down from the rush of adrenaline. His eyes slowly lower to the smoking Colt .45 in his hand. Many thoughts now raced through Bode's head. It had all happened so fast His natural survival instincts took over. His gun had once again become a mere extension of his body and mind. Everything he had tried to leave behind, it all came rushing back in one split second. The familiar rush of adrenaline, the feel of the trigger, the smell of gun smoke, it was like an old friend come to visit. The result of his relapse was three men dead by his hand. This is what Bode Johnson sought to escape from, death and guilt by his gun. In the moments that followed Bode Johnson felt a different strange sensation wash over him. He begins drawing in short but deep breaths. His eyes began to water up. He was experiencing a new feeling, one that he had not felt in some time. He tried to remember what it was called. Then it came to him.
It was remorse.

It had been so long since he had felt any emotion when it came to killing another man. The realization hit him like a rushing bull and took his wind from his gut He stood up, took in a deep breath and wiped at his eye, staring at the wetness on the tip of his finger. He looked past his hand to the bloody prone body of Brock Cody.

"Why?" he thought to himself. "Everything I've tried to accomplish here, all of it is gone now because of a gun!" Johnson throws away his pistol in disgust. He wipes his chin with the back of his hand as he stares down at Cody.

"Damn, Bode," said Jimmie Nevin in a hushed shocked tone as he joined Johnson over Cody's corpse. "I ain't never seen nothing like that in all my born days."

Bode could not take his eyes off Cody's bloodstained body.

"Four men . . . you took out all four men. Wildest shootin' I ever seen!

Nevin's astonishment was abruptly halted. Johnson grabbed him by his collar yanking him off his horse to the ground. Jimmie stumbles for his footing a bit but soon had his legs back under him, all the while in Bode's firm grasp.

"You think this is something to be proud of?" Bode shouts. Jimmie is frozen with shock at the tone and anger in Johnson's voice.

"Four men are dead! Dead, Jimmie! They are never going to see another sunrise. They are never going to get to kiss their wives or girlfriends again. All they get now is a plot of land and some words spoken over them. We are going to go back to town and go on with our lives but these men.

They are going to their graves Jimmie do you understand that. The damnation of the whole thing is that this did not need to happen!
I it did and I killed them! That's a hell of a burden to live with, kid, a hell of a burden!"

Bode turns loose his grip on Jimmie's shirt and sinks down on one knee. Jimmie backs away, straightens out his shirt and speaks in a hushed voice.

"Sorry Bode, it needed to be done, Bode. It was not murder. It was self-defense. Cody drew first, I seen him." Bode stood up and looked at the bodies of the four dead men laying strewn about the prairie grounds.

"Guess it doesn't matter who drew first now, does it?"

Bode, Jimmie and Charlie gather the bodies and tie them onto their respective horses, in tow riding them back to the ranch.

Bode tells the story of what had happened in the prairie to the ranch owner Randy Reeder. Charley and Jimmie were ordered to take the bodies into town and turn them over to the undertaker.

Bode asked Randy "Take me into the Marshal's office and let's explain it to him, we have to report this legally. I would guess that he would want to make a report and determine if there needs to be a court hearing on it."

Randy agreed and told Jimmie and Charlie to meet them at the Marshal's office with the bodies first. "Tell him we will be on our way in to file a report on the rustling of my cattle?"

In the weeks to come, Bode would be vindicated of murder by the court. Sitting right in the front row as the verdict was handed down was none other than Eric Desmond. Not guilty was the judgment by the jury. Eric Desmond just glared at Johnson as the words rang out in the courtroom. The townsfolk cheered and applauded at the decision. Eric Desmond just sat there and stared at Bode who returned the stare back. Both men knew there would be another encounter and because of that, one of them would die. Eric Desmond rose from his seat and placed his hat upon his head, never once taking his gaze from Bode. He left by the courtroom's center aisle and out the courthouse doors into the hot afternoon sun.

Following the trial, the townspeople quickly labeled Johnson a real hero based on the ever-growing story of what happened out there on the plains that day. The story was told many times over beers and whiskey and soon the story grew in intensity and with some exaggerations.

While Bode shunned the notoriety of being a local legend, he did however enjoy the opportunities, which were borne from the event just months after the shoot out with Brian Desmond, by the insistence of many of the townspeople, Bode ran for Town Marshal.

The town's former lawman, Marshal Ernie Braden, had ridden off in pursuit of two bank robbers, Garth Malone and Brant Nolan but had never returned. Rumor had it that all three were killed in a shootout near El Paso. That was over four months ago. The Deputy, a young headstrong kid, Denis Coughlan, handled the office

Braden's absence until the elections. He was hoping to be elected himself to Marshal.

At the election, the voting was a landslide in Bode's favor. Bode Johnson was sworn in October 1886 as the new Marshal of Steele Creek, Texas.
Denis Coughlan accepted Bode's offer to remain on as his deputy. Mica was never more proud of him.

As the time pass Bode found that, he was slowly fitting into the town's community and he was thoroughly embracing this new life. For the first time in a very long time, he felt a part of something meaningful. He thought about others before thinking of himself. He had finally let go of his past life and the sins contained therein. He was finally becoming the man he had always wanted to be.

CHAPTER 8

August 8, 1887
Sixty miles south of San Antonio

Nearing sundown James rode Argo up into a canyon and up to an old miner's cabin; he called out to the cabin. "Hello is there anyone home inside?"

"Who wants to know?" came his reply from inside, the man not showing himself near the door or windows.

"Texas Ranger, James McCloud! I am just passing through and seen some shelter in this place, might be a cool evening to sleep outside."

The door swung open as Johnny stepped out, "Would that be the same James McCloud, I rode with down Nogales way last season?"

"I be the same man, Johnny Hawk how have you been doing?"

"Well as Sheriff of Nogales I go by just John Hawk now, get on down from that horse and come on inside where we can catch up old friend."

John had already began fixing himself some beef stew and offered some to James. "I thank you for the kind offer and would like to sweeten your supper with some biscuits from Dallas and we can finish it off with this apple pie I brought along too. That is if you like pie?" said James.
The two of them caught up on the past year and finished off the pie with the coffee brewing over the fire stove, turning in early.

STEELE CREEK

Morning daybreak was beginning to hit the high slopes of the canyon, when James awakened he looked out through the open window and, watched the sun come up he could see that the morning was crisp and cool with a bit of frost on the grass.

The Mountains in the distance were magnificent peaks standing white capped with snow, silhouetted against a bright blue morning sky with hues of bright reds, pink, and light purple. He knew this was going to be a great start to the day but the skies warned of afternoon storms.

"You ready John? James asked, "It looks like rain today so you should pack your Slicker so it is easier to reach when it starts pouring." They went out and saddled the horses. John had been very careful at tucking everything in tight on Bo's saddlebags then draped his Slicker over the rear of the saddle cinching it down with the leather straps. James shared a few of the remaining molasses and oats with Johns horse Bo before they rode out.

By mid afternoon, the skies darkened suddenly. Another hour along the ride a cooler breeze swept across the trail with the scent of rain. The trail was now climbing upwards toward Devil's Rock and they could see off to the west the every growing grayish blue just peaking over the mountains. Bo's ears began twitching around sensing the impending storm, while Argo seems to remain calm. John Hawk reached down and patted Bo on the neck trying to assure him and keep him calm.

"I don't get it you said Argo senses danger long before you do but he hasn't even acknowledged this storm approaching!"

"Oh, but he has. We have been out on the plains and in the mountains for many years now and he knows how far and how fast this storm is coming. He is gonna take it in a little slower and is making sure he can get me along to a safer spot we can both shelter in."

Watching as they rode they knew that the sky would be opening up soon with a deluge of rain starting high in the mountains and rapidly rolling down on them as the ever so menacing clouds approached. They also realized that the rain in the mountains would be dumping the rain into the crevasses and ravines to wash down on them in torrents of rushing water, mud, and debris. They plodded along a more slowly watching for any flash flooding headed their way, both had pulled out their oiled skin slickers and put them on just as the cloud overhead opened up on them and the trail. The mud of the trail now slick with the rain loosened some of the small rock causing the horses to pick their footing more carefully. As they rounded, the next ridged the mountains to their right dropped off first gently and then more steeply as they rode ahead at this time Argo was moving more to the left side of the trail to stay closer to the mountain slope rising up on that side. John did not have to encourage Bo to follow, Bo instinctively tucked himself and John in closer to the inside edge. Pulling their hats down lower on their heads and letting the water runoff the brims and not down their necks, they plunged on ahead hugging the left side rocks sometimes even rubbing against the rock face on the left. As Argo stepped up his speed a little just enough to be ahead of Bo and John, he stopped and turned around.

John heard it too, "Is that Thunder?"
James now facing John said, "No, it's the beating of horse hooves in a gallop coming up the trail from behind you! Quick move up ahead and pull in as close as you can to the first area where the trail widens, quick first wide spot… hug the wall?"

Just as they got in as close as they could and under a rocky overhang nearly twenty men on horseback galloped past them. None had noticed McCloud or Hawk next to the wall tucked in behind, where a steady waterfall coming from the mountain above had hidden them from view.

Besides it was out of the rain altogether behind the overhang and they decided to wait there for a few more minutes.

"What do you think those men were up to?" asked John.

"By the size of the group and their willingness to break a horses leg and possibly their own necks from a fall on the rain slick rocks. I would say that they are either a Posse or they're riding into town to cause some breaking of the law or other unfortunate mischief!"

"Well, I didn't see any one ahead of them trying not to be caught, so I would bet on the last statement."

The rain had slowed some between the break in the clouds but would again pick up heavy soon, so they ducked out from under the overhang and picked up along the trail behind the gang of men whom had just passed.

Ranger McCloud and John rode into Steele Creek at about dusk and on through town until they reached the Marshal's office. McCloud pulled up the reigns and dismounted, Johnny followed as they tied off at the rail leaving enough slack that the horses could drink from the trough. When they reached the door, it was locked and there was only one oil lamp turned down very low inside. McCloud pounded on the door thinking either the Marshal or his Deputy was in the back room probably sleeping or that they were out checking up on things somewhere in town.

"Well I hadn't noticed any large groups of horses around anywhere as we rode in. Therefore, the Marshal most likely is not dealing with them yet. McCloud stated.

Johnny responded, "Maybe the Marshal went down to the saloon for an evening drink or just rattling the merchant's doors. What you say we check the Saloon first and wash some of this mud down my dry throat?"

James chuckled, "Sure maybe at least someone will

know where the Marshal is, a Saloon is the second best place to find out the town's gossip."

CHAPTER 9

'Troubadour from above'

Music and song, It has been said that its harmonious sounds can soothe even the most savage beast. Its words and tunes can brighten the most darkened heart or cause a tear to be shed almost at will. It is believed that music can even heal the afflicted with just a song. History is filled with tales of the sick and infirmed, once condemned to a sad fate, being cured just by listening to a soothing melody.

Music can also tell a story, a tale, which has many interpretations by both the musician and the listener alike. In medieval times a man known as a minstrel would travel the lands sharing his tunes and ballads for all who would listen. In this time and place there are modern-day minstrels known simply as troubadours; wandering musicians whose sole purpose is to entertain and amuse those who seek something more than just the weary notes of daily life here in the West.

Such an individual is about to enter town and in doing so, enter the very lives of those therein. The messages of his melodic refrains will most assuredly impact those who would listen to his tuneful ballads. He comes with a purpose to provide music, merriment and more for one and all with merely a guitar in hand and a saddlebag full of hopes and dreams on his back.

However, he is not the only music-maker who has come to town. Another plays a different tune that does not take wishes or desires for your songs. Their melodic paths will undoubtedly cross in a crescendo of fates with the final note yet to be written.

Therefore, everyone should take heart for 'The Troubadour' has come to town and he will most definitely being taking your requests.

From his office door, Marshal Bode Johnson stared out into the early morning bustle of Main Street and rubbed his aching right wrist.

"Damn this weather" he said through clenched teeth as he glanced down at the painful joint.

It was just one of many physical mementos from a past encounters which always bothered him on damp days and today looked to have a storm coming in. As he stood, the he casually observed the pulse of the town. A man dressed all in white complete with white bowler hat steps off the early stagecoach. He motions for his luggage, which apparently consists of a simple square case. Johnson shakes his head in amusement and chuckles at the sight of such a dandy.

His gaze then turns to the front of the Brazos Hotel where the usual gang of gossiping hens gathers to deliberate about the latest buzz in the social scene. He then shifts his gaze to the North end of Main Street when a figure catches his eye. He watches with curious interest as a smallish man makes his way down the avenue walking with obvious deliberation aside his grey and black burro.

At first glance, he appeared to be a Mexican farmer, dressed in the usual white shirt, short pants with rope belt and sandals. Atop his head sat a straw sombrero with a shiny silver band around it. The man's head was hung low as if a heavy weight were about his shoulders causing him labored steps as he walked.

Such transients often made their way here. Some stayed on with purpose while others had their purpose motivate them to leave. However, Johnson sensed there was something a little different about this wanderer and he wanted to find out just what his gut was telling.

"Hola, mi amigo" Johnson calls out to the man in his best Spanish dialect. He had picked up quite a bit of the language from his years roaming the border towns as a running gun. Sometimes it came in very handy to speak the native tongue when avoiding that Icon reach of the Long Arm of the Law.

The man stops and lifts the brim of his hat to see who is addressing him. He has a forlorn look about his face. The man's eyes then make their way to the shiny five-point star on Johnson's chest. The traveler's face now lights up with a smile. He walks his burro over to the lawman with a bit more spring in his step.

"Buenos Dias, señor," the man said with an enthusiasm previously unseen. "Como estas?"

"Muy Bueno" Johnson notices a shiny silver cross around his neck. "You speak English?"

"Si, Si . . . yes, I speak ingles", he replies nodding his head rapidly.

"Good, good. What's your name, friend?"

"Me Nombre? I'm sorry señor, my name is Lucio" he replies humbly but with bright eyes. His Boyish smile is almost infectious.

"What brings you to our little town?"

The man pauses briefly then holds up a finger. He turns to his burro and removes a plain wooden guitar, displaying it to the marshal with a wide smile.

"I am a trovador, señor!" he said boldly.

"A what? You mean a 'troubadour' like a . . . a traveling singer?"

"Exactamente, amigo!" he said excitedly. "I am a- a troubadour . . . but not just any troubadour, no, amigo. I am el trovador Del dios."

"A troubadour . . . from God?" queries Johnson with a look of bemused confusion.

"Si! I roam the land with a song for everyone, señor."

"Everyone, eh?" said Johnson with a half smile and a chuckle.

"Si, señor! Would you like me to sing you a song?" he said with gleeful anticipation.

"Well I don't …"

"Please, it would be no trouble," insists the man.

Johnson nods his acceptance and the little man begins lightly strumming his guitar.

> ♪*"In the land of suns and shadows is a man,*
> *Whose heart is brave and wise,*
> *He wear a star upon his breast,*
> *For those with evil eyes*
> *He stand for law and righteousness*
> *He accept no sinful deed*
> *His soul was once a blackened spot*
> *But now is holy cleaned*
> *He fight for justice and for God*
> *A long life he should lead*
> *For he is a man of true belief*
> *Señor Johnson. . . was. . . indeed."*♪

Lucio stops playing and wiggles his right hand as if trying to loosen it from discomfort.

Johnson smiled and nodded his head in quiet approval.

"Muy Bueno, my friend, Muy Bueno" he said with a few claps of endorsement. You are very good!

"Gracias, señor" replies the man taking off his sombrero with a bow. He pauses there in calmness his eyes slowly glancing up to Johnson's in obvious expectation.

The man coughs and winces slightly.

Johnson soon understands the expectation and nods. He reaches into his shirt pocket, removing a silver dollar and dropping it into the sombrero.

"Mucho gracias, señor" said the man removing the coin from the hat and placing the sombrero back upon his head. He turns the coin side-to-side, examining it closely with one eye and smiles.

"Can you tell me where I can get a room and a meal?"

"Sure. Head on down to the Steele Point. They will fill your belly right. As for a room, try Miss. Veolia's, She runs a boarding house down on Second St.

Tell her I sent you," Johnson said with a wink.

"Gracias aguín, señor" said Lucio. He then coughs again clutching his chest.

"You okay, Lucio?" asks Johnson eyeing the agony on the minstrel's face.

"Si, Si, señor" he replies in exhausted breath. "I fear it is just a lingering malady from my journey here. I will be alright."

Lucio slings his guitar onto his back and leads his burro away.

Johnson smiles to himself as he ponders the song just played for him. He mutters the final line in an off-key tone.

"Señor Johnson was indeed."

He shakes his head in happy perplexity as he turns back into his office. He suddenly stops in his tracks and spins back around on his heels.

"Hey! How would you know…" his voice trails off as he realizes the man's out of sight, "… my name?"

Johnson removes his hat and scratches the top of his head. He replaces the hat, shrugs his shoulders in resignation and walks back into his office.

Where did this man come from, who is he and what does he really know? Bode was again agitated with himself. He is just a simple man, surely not any threat to me.

CHAPTER 10

LeAnn Weavers hunched over a bucket of feed inside her chicken pen. She wiped her brow with a dirty handkerchief and glanced up at the mid-morning sun. She was already exhausted from the long list of chores she had been completing. Life on a farm, even a meager one such as hers, is a demanding one.

Life has been hard on her since her husband had passed away two years ago. He was a lunger and suffered with the consumption mightily before crossing over. LeAnn caring for and watching the love her life wither away took its toll on her emotionally as well as physically. She could have packed up and moved back to her folks' ranch in Colorado but she was never one take the easy route. Instead, she fought to keep her farm and make a go of it raising cows, chickens and pigs. She tends a vegetable garden as well to help provide meals.

The one thing that her husband's tragedy did do for her is to harden her for a life out here in the West. She knew she had to be strong even in the wake of tragedy not just for her own self-preservation but also for Chester, her six-year-old son.

"I'll feed them, momma!" hollers Chester as he runs to the pen.

LeAnn beams a warm smile.

"You go make me some more lemonade," he said with a wide grin "please?"

LeAnn ruffles the curly red locks on Chester's head.

"You remember now, don't give them too much or they'll get so fat we won't be able to haul to the barn in the fall"

"I remember, momma" he replies with certainty in his tone.

LeAnn smiles again and heads for the house. There is a noticeable limp in her gate as she makes her way through the sparsely grassed front yard. Her journey is suddenly interrupted by a familiar voice.

"You still lamed up, LeAnn?"

She spins around and a smile again brightens her face.

"Good morning Marshal," she said wiping off her hands on the handkerchief.

Bode Johnson walks through the small wooden gate and removes his hat.

"You look like you're hobbling even worse than the other day. I cannot believe your foot not healed by now. What has it been now? Must be a couple weeks anyhow," he said with concern in his voice.

LeAnn's eyes lower to the ground before raising them to meet Johnson.

"Well, truth be told it's actually a month now" she said sheepishly.

"A month?" said Johnson in surprise. "What's Doc say?"

LeAnn gives a nervous glance towards the chickens. Johnson's gaze follows suit as they watch little Chester feed the chickens. Johnson returns his eyes to the lady.

"LeAnn? Is everything alright?"

"Please" she said with sadness in her voice, "my apology come inside."

They enter the modest home and LeAnn shows Johnson to the kitchen where she can look out the window and still see Chester in the pen. She continues watching him as she speaks in a somber tone.

"I saw doc just the other day. I told him it still bothers

me and the wound seems to be festering worse. He looked at it and. . . . " she raised a frail trembling hand to her eyes. Clearly fighting tears, she continued.

"He said it's not just an infection. He said it is some disease, which gets in and takes root. He said he read about it when he was out east at some medical school. He said once it's rooted into the muscle and bone there's no curing it."

Softly she begins to cry never taking her eyes off her son.

"Is there anything he can…?"

"No" she said firmly. "He said that within a month or so . . . oh Bode, he describes a horrible fate."

She finally breaks down and buries her face in Johnson's chest. He places an arm gently around her shoulder to comfort her.

"He said once the wound turns black its taken root. It takes over the body and death surely follows."

"Well lemme have a look," he said.

LeAnn sits down at the kitchen table and removes the bandages from her left foot. Bode squats down and holds the heel of her foot in his hand. He glances at the wound on the bottom of her foot He studies for a second or two then raises his eyes to hers. The flesh surrounding the wound has taken on a bluish-black hue.

"Let's get a fresh dressing on this," he said in a noncommittal manner as if merely dressing a scratched knee of a child.

After applying a new wrap, Bode draws in a Deep breath.

"Look it could just need to…"

LeAnn interrupts him.

"Don't try and sugarcoat it, Bode. I know it's blackened. I also know what that means."

She begins crying again.

"LeAnn, I'm sure if we took you up to El Paso that the doctor there might be able to help."

"I'm not worried for me, Bode," she said frantically wiping away the tears from her face. Through teary eyes, she looks into Bode's eyes. "What's going to happen to Chester?"

Marshal Bode Johnson has no answer for all questions. All he can do is provide a shoulder to comfort LeAnn Weavers' heartache.

LeAnn continues to weep a few more minutes before gathering herself. "I was making Chester some lemonade may I offer you some Marshal?"

"Now don't go all formal on me, continue to call me Bode, and yes I would love some lemonade!"

After he finished the glass and had spoken with Chester on how big he was getting, and how much help he was to his mother. He said, "I hope to see you both in church on Sunday and if you need anything be sure to let me know?"

CHAPTER 11

"I said give me another bottle or so help me Grayson, I'll fill this bar with holes from top to bottom!" barked the burly hunk of a man known to all as "The Lightning," or "El Relampago" in Spanish, Milan Rodriquez.

Rodriquez was a surly deeply tanned man who would rather end a dispute with a bullet instead of words. He was a hard man, made harder from years inside a Mexican prison as the story has it. It is said that he was a scout for the US Army when tracking raiding Apache and Comanche Indians during 'The First Battle of Adobe Walls' where he was known as a particularly savage individual with a lust for brutality as strong as his lust for liquor. He was put in prison because of his 'over zealous' efforts to subdue the Indians particularly the women and children.

That was nearly twenty years ago when he was an angry young man of eighteen.
He spent five years confined to a dingy cell and when he got out all that had been accomplished by his incarceration was to make him a more vicious, ill-tempered killer, he roamed the Southwest, looting, rustling and if you believe the stories, taking lives without regret or remorse courtesy of his quick draw. The tales of his lightning fast reflexes spread throughout the territory and he became a fiercely dreaded man. He wandered the land

because of wanderlust or necessity leaving ugliness and fear in his wake.

Now here in Hank Grayson's Forty Rivers Saloon, he is in a foul mood undeniably.

"I'm not gonna ask again, Dumbass!" he bellows brandishing his army Colt revolver for all to see. He slams it down on his table.

"Here! Here!" said Hank Grayson, proprietor of the establishment. "Take the bottle and go!"

Almost instantly, Rodriquez's demeanor shifts to one of smug arrogance at the acquiescence of Grayson to his demand.

"There! You see my friends how simple it is to get service when you know the right way to ask," he said smiling, his yellow-brown teeth providing a less than appealing sight. He pulls the cork from the bottle with his teeth but his drinking is quickly disturbed by sharp pain across the top of his head.

THUD!

Rodriquez slumps over from the impact toppling both he and his chair to the grimy barroom floor in a cloud of dust. The dazed vaquero winces and squints up at dispense of his anguish, Marshal Bode Johnson.

"What the . . . ?" he said in a groggy haze.

Johnson had just buffaloed El Relampago from behind.

"Just stay right there, Mr. Rodriquez, I'll be with you in a minute" said Johnson in that calm but firm take charge tone of voice reserved for intense situations such as these.

Johnson grabs a few silver coins from the table and tosses them to Grayson who stands in front of the bar.

"That about cover him?" he asks the anxious owner.

Grayson nods and now Johnson takes Rodriquez' Colt and sticks it barrel-first into his trousers' waist.

"Denis, you go clear a cell for Mr. Rodriquez here. He'll be joining us tonight for supper," he said motioning towards the front doors with his head. "Now then Mr. Rodriquez, you are under arrest for disturbing the peace, public intoxication and anything else I can come up with along the way to the jail. Let's go."

Johnson reaches down, grabs a handful of the semiconscious rogue's shirt, and drags him up to his feet with a degree of awkwardness on Rodriquez's part naturally. Out in the street the pair went… Rodriquez staggering, holding onto his lumped noggin and the Marshal leading him along by the collar.

It made quite the sight for the townsfolk meandering along Main Street in the late afternoon. Most had waited out the rain in some shop or bar, but now that the sun was shining, again they were back moving about town.

A good twenty minutes later James McCloud and Johnny arrived at the saloon and entered seeking out the far end of the bar, furthest away from the door in view of the entire place. John Hawk had ordered up his second beer when he asked the bartenders name.

"My name is Hank Grayson proprietor of the Forty Rivers Saloon here who may I ask is wanting to know?"

"Well I am John Hawk a Nogales lawman and this is Texas Ranger, James McCloud."

"A Texas Ranger named McCloud you say, the Marshal was in here not to long ago, sez if I had heard that you came into town, to send you down to the Marshal's Office at the end of town square."

James ordered another beer thinking that the Marshal was out earlier and it is indicated he went back there, most likely now having dinner maybe we should eat before going on to his office. "Is there a place you would recommend for some vittles?" asked McCloud.

Hank replied, "At this time of night I would recommend Miss Veolia's she runs a boarding house and diner down on Second St. So if you need a room she most likely can take care of that too!"

"What time does she stop serving dinner?" James asked.

"She most likely closes her kitchen at Ten p.m. but she has been known to feed the weary traveler much later, if she is willing and she is not to awfully tired."

"Well let's see it is now Seven p.m. so I think we could have a few more drinks then head over there and check in.," said John.

They stood at the end of the bar farthest away from the door as usual and scanned the room.

The table next to the piano player was full with eight men player a round of cards. John glanced over at them and noticed that the one player was none other than Kendall Caruthers, from St. Louis. John turned his attention back to the bartender and asked. "The man seated at the table in the black vest and white shirt, has he been here long?"

"Him, he arrived yesterday and has taken every farmer and cowhand that has tried to play him? He has won every hand so far and it doesn't look like he is going to lose this one either?"

McCloud asked, "What is it John do you know who he is?"

"Yep, that is Mr. Caruthers from up in St. Louis, I believe he goes by Kendall Caruthers, a card hustler from way back, he plays a few hands losing, until he reals in the big players then he takes them for what they have. It has never been proven but most think he has a pretty good slight of hand when he plays."

"You don't say?" mentioned McCloud. "Maybe I would like to play him a hand or two, just to see how he plays?"

McCloud waited until someone folded and threw down his cards leaving, empty of his monthly earnings as a cowhand.

"Would you mind if I sat in on the next deal?" asked James.

The men nodded with one saying, "If you are willing to put up the starting pot opening of two hundred we will accept your offer to join us!"

"Seems like a good starting point," as James reached into his vest pocket he retrieved a bundle of dollars bills and placed them on the table. He counted out the two hundred and set it aside, putting the rest back inside his vest. Being the new player at the table, he won the first three hands without any trouble. He thought for sure he was being fed the right cards from the dealer Kendall Caruthers. However, there was no way he had noticed any defaults in the dealing of the cards.

Kendall had a sharp eye out for whom ever he played, to read them trying to find any clues to their facial expressions body posture or fidgeting to indicate to him on what they were hiding or possibly holding in the cards.

He was dressed in black leather vest and a crisp white shirt with a high stiff collar wearing four rings, one gold and one silver on each hand. The gold ones each adorned a large diamond embedded in the center and paired with smaller ruby's beside it. His dark eyes were a match to his slick black hair. James had noticed the three ladies admiring him at the next table sure, that at least one of them would follow him later back to his room.

John order himself another beer and getting one to deliver to McCloud at the table. The others at the table were all drinking whiskey poured into their glasses from one of the two clay bottles on the table.

Ron Graziano sitting across from James stopped the game for a moment and asked, "That personal assistant you have is not trying to pass you any information as to what cards we might be holding, now is he?"

"Mr. Hawk here is not a personal assistant he is just a friend of mine refreshing my beer nothing else to it, sir." That brought out a short laugh from the players as they continued with the hand at play. The cards were dealt in a prearranged combination of the facedown and face-up rounds, with a round of betting following each. They were dealt one card at a time, facedown, with a betting round between each, being that they were playing seven-card stud, Kendall dealt two extra cards to each player.

Graziano was holding the ten, nine, eight and seven of clubs it was his ante. Ron smiled and tossed a few silver dollar on the pot raising the stakes. Everybody passed out up to McCloud. He matched filling in the pot and drew a card.

Caruthers was the only other stayer as he stared; drew a cigar slowly from his pocket placing it between his teeth and placed on the table James' match.

The table fell to a complete silence around the green-clothed table. Graziano was studying his hand with a kind of contemptuous smile, but in his eyes there perhaps was to be seen a cold, stern light expressing something sinister and relentless.

Caruthers sat as he had sat. As the pause grew longer, he looked up once inquiringly at the older man Graziano.

The old man reached down on the floor for two wheel nuts from his new wagon outside. "Well, mine are worth about that much," said he, tossing it into the pot. He leaned back comfortably in his chair and renewed his stare at the five straight clubs.

McCloud fingered his bills and looked pensively at his hand. The silence of those moments plagued Caruthers like the smoke from a brushfire.

McCloud continued for some moments coolly observing his cards. At last, he breathed a little sigh and said, "Well, Mr. Graziano, looks like this game just turned to 'Nuts', I can't play a sure thing against you." He threw in Eight Silver dollars as his match. "I'll just call you. I've got only two pair." He placed down his cards they were two pair of eights, four eights. The 'Nuts' James was referring to was that Graziano had bet his wagon on the game, and by placing the wheel nuts on the table it insured he would not be able to run out on the game and ride away.

Graziano's fear, horror, and rage could only be equaled in volume to a small explosion of TNT. He dashed his cards upon the table. "There!" he shouted, glaring at Kendall. "I've got a straight flush, and it is Jack high!"

Graziano was reaching for the pot when Caruthers tossed in his coins to the pot, and drew his last card from the deck. "You might want to hold a minute there, I have something to show you!" As he laid down a royal flush, hearts Ace high."

Graziano was broken, as he stared at the cards on the table and then to the large pot with two of his wagon wheel nuts. He stood quickly to walk away knocking his chair over banging it on the floor. He was halfway to the door when he stopped, drawing his Ivory handled Colt from its holster on his hip. John was quicker but not at drawing, he had slipped up behind Graziano and smashed the thick beer mug over his head dropping him to the floor.

Caruthers had been watching Graziano as he walked towards the door and had jumped up and drew his own pistol aiming it at Graziano. James threw a blocking arm up catching Kendall's elbow as the gun fired into the ceiling.

McCloud had Caruthers sit back down as he held his Colt .45 on him. John was reviving Graziano and had him seated in another chair near the bar. The patrons who had all, either ducked or ran to the backside of the bar were now coming back to their tables. The piano player had stopped playing but stayed seated on the floor beside the upright large wooden piano.

"Now Ranger you seen what happened here he was the first to draw on me. I had the rights to defend myself?"

James picked up the remaining undealt deck of cards on the table and flipped through them finding a second Ace, and a second King of Hearts.

"To me Mister Caruthers it seems as the dealer in this game you have obviously palmed a few extra cards into your hand making you the presumed winner."

"You're telling me he has been cheating us all night?" Ron Graziano said rubbing his head.

Johnny had to hold him down in his seat to keep him from going for Caruthers again.

Ron's throat seemed filled with pounded glass. "Pass the whisky. My head is killing me, did you have to hit me so hard."

John looked at him saying, "Sorry Sir, it was better than you shooting him or getting shot yourself, after all you were the one stealing their money all evening!" James opened his vest to reveal the Texas Ranger Star.

"I must arrest you and turn you over to the town Marshal Mr. Caruthers!"

John Hawk stepped up to the table showing his Sheriff's badge. He began sorting the money on the table. After that is was returned to the rightful owners, accounting for where they had stood at their last hand. Holding some back for the man who had just left the bar. John turned that amount over to the bartender, "I am sure that you will see to it he gets something back?"

James sorted Caruthers' pile of cash dividing it up between them leaving Kendall only twenty dollars, for his bail if, and when the Marshal decided bail was an option.

Marshal Bode Johnson locked Caruthers into the cell next to Rodriquez and sat down to hear the story of the Gambler.

James, John and Bode shared the stories of the two cellmates and then moved on to the real reason McCloud had been assigned to come to Steele Creek, Texas.

Later they turned in at Miss Veolia's getting themselves two rooms. John rode the new 'Lift' while James refused and walked up the stairs. He still did not trust climbing inside a small box and being lifted to the next floors by ropes. John could hear him mumbling something about a man named 'OTIS.'

CHAPTER 12

Lucio drew in a heavy labored breath as he sat down on his bed. He had taken the Marshal's advice and rented a room at Miss Veolia's Boarding House with what little money he had left having just finished a big dinner at the Steele Point Diner; he was ready for a siesta. He swung his guitar, which traveled with him everywhere, around and off his shoulder. He walked over and placed it standing up in the corner of the room. He untied his rope belt and returned to the bed. He stretches and yawns as he slowly lays his head on the pillow.

Suddenly he heard a ruckus coming from outside his window. He sat up and moved the curtain aside. Down on the street he could see a Texas Ranger and another man drag their prisoner up the boulevard. Lucio gave a slight chuckle at the sight. He shut the curtain and lay back down on the bed in restful repose.

As he lay there staring at the ceiling, a smile appears on his face. It was a knowing smile. He was very happy that he had decided to come to this little town. His talent had drawn him to this place and he now knew that his talent would most certainly be of some use before his stay would end. He closed his eyes and said a short prayer under his breath before drifting off to sleep

"Chester! Chester!" LeAnn hollers out the back door towards the smallish grey barn about a hundred feet away.

She watches the open barn door with a furrowed brow. Sudden her face lights up as Chester appears in the doorway. He has something in his hand behind his back.

"Did you finish your chores?" she said firmly but with love in her voice.

"Yup" said Chester. "Close your eyes"

"What? Oh Chester I don't have time for foolishness" she said as she turns to enter the house.

"Momma, please" he begs. "Just close your eyes for a second"

She spins back to face him in the doorway, a smile on her lips.

"Are they closed, Momma?"

"Yup"

"Are they shut tight?"

"Yes now come on"

"Okay" he said bringing his hand out from behind his back. "You can open them now"

LeAnn opens her eyes and her smile grows wider. There in her little boy's hands was a bunch of wild flowers.

"You like 'em, momma?" he said with frantic enthusiasm.

"Nope" she said plainly without emotion.

A crestfallen Chester's jaw drops at the sentiment.

"I love them," LeAnn said squatting down and holding her arms out for him. He practically runs to her embrace.

"I picked them special for you," he said in her ear. "Just like Daddy used to do."

"Thank you," she softly replies in his ear tears in her eyes. "Now you go wash up because suppers ready."

"What's for supper?"

"Chicken soup and some homemade sweetbread with strawberry jam," she said cupping his freckled face in her left hand.

"Oh goody!" he said with excitement. "Will we be going to Auntie Vee's for breakfast tomorrow?"

"Well tomorrow is Saturday so what do you think?"

she said as she tussles his red hair once more.

"I think I like her strawberry jam too," he said with a grin.

"Well then it's settled. We'll be eating breakfast with Auntie Vee," she said confidently. "Just like we do every Saturday, silly"

"Oh boy!" he said running off.

LeAnn slowly stands up and picks over the flowers in her grasp. She stiffens and blinks several times fighting back the flood of tears at the ready in her eyes. She gently holds the flowers to her chest, smiles and walks back into the kitchen. She retrieves a vase from the cupboard and placing the flowers in it, puts it on the table. She glances out the window beside the table and sees the pink and purple sky as the sun sets behind the mountains.

She wipes away a tear from her cheek and smiles. Later she would tend to her wound then cry herself to sleep again.

CHAPTER 13

"Hey!" the growly voice beckoned from beyond the wood plank door.
Marshal Bode Johnson sat at his desk mulling over a stack of wanted posters as if he never heard a thing.

"Marshal! I know you're out there!" the voice snarled. "You plan on starving' me to death?"
Without acknowledgement, Johnson stood up and walked over to the potbelly stove in the front corner of the room. He pours himself a cup of coffee and sips it while glancing out the barred window. Then suddenly a slight grin creases his lips. He walks back over to the desk and looks down at the wanted poster splayed on the desk. He shuffles couple around as he takes another sip. The silence is broken by a knock on the door.

"It's open," said Bode as he singlehandedly begins gathering the posters into a pile like a deck of playing cards and straightens them out.

The door opens and in steps Bode's wife, Mica. In her arms is a large tray covered by a red gingham cloth. Bode smiles at the sight.

"I thought you and your new boarders might enjoy some supper," she said setting the tray upon the large oak desk.

She pulls the cloth off the meals with a confident grin like a magician's assistant.

"Three steak dinners complete with the trimmings," she said triumphantly.

Bode cups her face in his hands and looks into her eyes, grinning all the while.

"I love you, Mrs. Johnson," he said planting a little kiss on her lips. "I'm as hungry as a newborn cub"

"Well now, if that's just for a dinner I can't wait for breakfast" she replies with a sparkle in her eye.

"Marshal? Marshal!" the gruff voice barks out once more from beyond the door to the cells. Both Mica and Bode glance at the door then back at each other once again.

"Well I've got to get back to the diner. The supper crowd's starting to pour in.," she said rubbing Bode's arms with her hands.

Bode nods in slight resignation. As Mica approaches the front door, she looks back over her shoulder.

"I'll see you tonight, Mr. Johnson." She said playfully and then disappears out the door.

Bode shakes his head and chuckles to himself he gathers two plates of food. He takes a deep whiff and his smile grows a little wider in anticipation. He walks to the back room door and takes down the large set of keys hanging on the wall beside it. He unlocks the wooden door and walks in.

Inside the back room are three cells, one large cell to the right and two smaller individual cells on the left. Bode's guests are located in the last two cells on the left and Rodriquez is waiting to greet the marshal with a nasty scowl and a very ugly disposition.

"'Bout time you feed me, Mister!" he growls through his stained teeth.

"It's Marshal, my friend and if you keep bumping' your gums in that tone this just might be your last meal" Bode said calmly but looking the man right in his eyes.

There was no mistaking the meaning behind the words. Rodriquez knew this and settled his temper just a bit all the while know that the law couldn't hold him for long and when he was free then he'd deal with this lawman who has wronged him.

"Let's see what passes for a meal in this crappy town," he grumbles.

Bode passes the metal plate through the slot in the cell door and into the eager hands of the outlaw. Rodriquez looks it over with what he feels is a discerning culinary eye before sitting on his bunk and eating.

"Not half bad," he said after a couple mouthfuls. "I mean, it ain't Delmonico's but it ain't bad"

Caruthers had remained quiet and began eating his steak without complaint he knew it best not stirring up problems with the man who had you locked away and the only person who would provide you water and food while locked away.

"Good. Enjoy it, you should be more like the Gambler here and keep your mouth shut." said Johnson turning to leave.

"Hey. . . Marshal" said Rodriquez in a sarcastic tone. Johnson stops and turns his head to look back at his prisoner.

"You can't hold me here forever," Rodriquez said ominously with a greasy grin.

Johnson smiles.

"And none of us live forever either?" said Johnson.

The greasy grin quickly disappears from the bandit's lips as Johnson turns and shuts the door behind him.

CHAPTER 14

The smell of steak and eggs wafted into the room and licked at Lucio's nose. He drew in a deep breath and smiled. He sat up and swung his feet around to the floor. He stretched his arms out tightly as a yawn came over him. He took another deep breath and knew breakfast was calling him. He grabs his guitar from its corner resting place and heads downstairs.

He turns at the bottom of the stairs and follows the delicious aroma down a short hallway and through an open doorway on the left. There seated at a dining table were four other people. At another sat two tall men, Ranger McCloud and Sheriff Johnny Hawk. Scattered around the room where another eight or so men all at different tables of two.

James McCloud had quietly pointed out their very muddy clothes and boots, now drying and leaving clumps falling loose to the floor around their feet.

"I'd say they are a few of those that rode through yesterday in the large group, and most likely the ones the Marshal has been warned about." Replied John.

On the left end of the first table sat a rotund man with a balding noggin, beady little eyes and three chins, who was shoveling hotcakes into his mouth as if he stole them. Seated next to him is a young woman dressed in a plain blue dress and wiping the mouth of the small boy seated next to her.

Lucio then looked at the man seated at the far right end of the table. He drew in a breath of surprise. The man was most certainly a dandy, dressed in a white suit, dark blue shirt and white bolo tie with a silver conch and turquoise stone in the center. He had very short but wavy silver hair, which crested on his crown in a combed back way; He was clean-shaven and immaculately groomed. Lucio glanced down at the floor beside the man. He knew what he was looking for and it was there, a black and silver case.

"Well Buenos Dias, señor" said Miss Veolia, mangling the dialect with a wide smile as she walks into the room holding a steaming pile of pancakes on a platter. "I wasn't sure you were going to make it down for breakfast Mr. Lucio. However, there is more than enough to go around. Please seat yourself anywhere"

Lucio nervously sat down as he looked at the man on the far right end of the long table.

"Oh where are my manners?" said Miss Veolia setting the plate of hotcakes in the center of the table, and then wiping her face with a red gingham cloth. "Let me introduce everyone. This is Mr. Alexander Corrigan. He is a lady's garment seller from Dodge City up in Kansas"

The chubby man smiles and nods with a tip of his steak-filled fork.

"Beside him is my sister, LeAnn and her son Chester," said Veolia.

LeAnn smiles and nods as she spreads some strawberry jam onto a piece of toast for her son.

"And this is Mr. Gabriel..."

"Gabriel Samuel Horne esquire, but please" the man interrupts, "call me Gabe."

"Everyone this is Lucio" said Miss Veolia.

The well-dressed man stands and extends his hand to Lucio with a telling smile. He is deeply tanned which contrasts heavily against his white outfit. He has eyes that at so pale blue that they almost appear white. Lucio stares into those eyes, then down to the square black and silver case on the floor next to his chair. The man follows Lucio's gaze down to the box and then back up to Lucio's face. He speaks with a very Eastern educated accent.

"You are a musician, are you not?" the man asks. Lucio does not answer. A bead of sweat trickles down the right side of his brow. He remains standing in the same spot, his gaze firmly fixed on Horne's entrancing alabaster eyes.

"Yes, well, I believe we have something in common, Mr. Lucio" Horne said withdrawing his hand awkwardly. Lucio's eyes widen at Horne's words as if some horrible truth were about to be revealed. . .

"You see," said Horne with a Cheshire catlike grin, "I sometimes play an instrument as well; the horn."

Lucio feels a lump in his throat as he swallows hard.

"Do I know you Lucio?" the man asks with a smile.

The question seems to jar Lucio out of his trance.

"Ah, no señor, I mean I don't think so but it's possible" he stammers nervously." I travel much. Perhaps we crossed paths in the past."

"Hmmm, I'm sure," said Gabriel. "Come, join us for breakfast." James and Johnny just watched them as they ate their breakfast continuing to talk about the reason they were there.

Slowly Lucio pulled out the wooden chair. He took his seat and smiled as LeAnn Weavers handed him a plate of eggs.

"Try these, they're delicious," she said.

"Ah, gracias, señorita" he replies as he stabs a couple eggs with his fork onto his plate. He nervously glances back at Samuel who is now reading the town's only newspaper, 'The Chronical'.

Lucio loads a couple flapjacks onto his plate, followed by a hunk of steak and begins eating, still casting an occasional concerned glance at Gabriel.

"Would you like another glass of milk, dear?"
The words seem to pull Lucio's attention to LeAnn Weavers and her son. The boy nods as LeAnn gets up from the table and makes her way into the kitchen. Lucio notices the obvious limp with which the young woman walks. He watches as she slightly drags her injured leg. His heart softens and a smile barely moves his lips. He looks to the boy who is engrossed in spreading strawberry jam all over his hands as well as the toast provided on his plate. He stifles a slight chuckle at the sight as another piece of flapjack enters his mouth. His mind is already at work crafting a song for her and her boy after all, he is a troubadour.

The moment is broken as LeAnn returns with a fresh glass of milk for her little man.

"Here you go," she said placing the milk on the table in front of him. Chester grasps the glass and begins gulping it down. Nearly finishing it, he sets down the glass revealing a milk moustache on his upper lip. Both he and LeAnn share a laugh over it.

Allow me said Gabe reaching over with a handkerchief to wipe the milk away.

A shiver goes up Lucio's spine. Gabriel sits back in his chair, neatly folding the handkerchief and placing upon the table. He leans back in his chair and smiles at Lucio.

Lucio swallows hard once again before wiping his own mouth. He had a very bad feeling about this Mr. Gabriel.

It was a feeling of fear of what was to come.

CHAPTER 15

While Kendall Caruthers remained locked up in his cell outside past the wooden door he heard.

"Where's my pistol?" Rodriquez growled as he stepped into the street outside the Marshal's office. Bode Johnson reached into his waistband and pulled out the Ivory handled Colt .45.

"You mean this?" said Johnson looking the gun piece over with disgust. "I think its best that I keep it."

"You ain't got the right," said Rodriquez taking a very purposeful step towards Johnson.

"Well, can't argue with a man who knows the law." Said Johnson with all the sarcasm he could muster. He tosses the pistol into the dirt at Rodriquez's feet.

"You really ought to clean that thing," he said, never taking his eyes off Rodriquez. "It's liable to misfire when you need it most."

Milan Rodriquez growls as he stares at Johnson. He reaches down and retrieves the grubby gun from its filthy resting place.

He blows about it trying to clear away some of the dust. He looks up to find Johnson still standing there eyeballing him hard.

A smile creeps onto Rodriquez's face.

"Some might say what I got here is an opportunity, amigo."

"That's right, friend" said Johnson stepping to the edge

of the boardwalk. "An opportunity for you to walk away while you still can!"

There is an awkward pause as Rodriquez licks his grimy smiling lips. The outlaw rolls the Colt chamber across his forearm with a firm eye.

His face distorted into an angry glare.

"You took all my bullets!" he bellows.

Marshal Bode Johnson allows a sly grin to crease the corner of his mouth.

"Don't make anymore trouble here, Rodriquez, or the next time I have your gun," he said in a terse low tone glancing up the street, "you'll be in the ground, Comprende?"

"Hah!" spits Rodriquez as he walks away in a huff.

Johnson watches as the outlaw meanders his way across Main Street to Front Street and disappears into Whiskey River Bar beside Doc Johnsen's office. He can tell that there is something in the air, something foreboding, and whatever it is . . . it is coming very soon.

CHAPTER 16

Lucio leans on his shoulder against the post in front the of Miss Veolia's Boarding House. He watches as LeAnn Weavers and her son cross Second Street. He again takes note the laboring limping steps of Mrs. Weavers. A voice from behind him speaks.

"It's tragic shame and it breaks my heart," the voice said.

Lucio turns his head to see Miss Veolia stand behind him watching the pair as well. She steps up beside him and they both continue to watch mother and son as they progress down the avenue.

"What is her affliction, Miss Veolia?" asks Lucio.

"She got an infection that has taken root in her leg. She cut her foot pretty badly about two months ago and she had it taken care of by Doc Johnsen."

"You mean the Marshal is a doctor also?" he asks quizzically.

"Oh heavens, no" she laughs slightly. "It's Doc Johnsen that is with an 'e-n on the end. The Marshal is 'o-n' on the end. No relation."

"Ah, Si, Si" replies Lucio returning his attention back the pair as they approach Main Street.

"Anyways, they thought she was doing fine but a couple of days ago they discovered the infection had already set in too deep for cleansing. They tried everything; axle grease, spider webs, nothing said its something called 'green gang' or 'ganglious green' or some such thing, I can't recall. Doc said he was schooled on it when he went back east a while ago for medical learning. The plain fact is Doc said she's got a terrible road ahead of her."

"What will happen to el pequeño, uh, to her little boy?" He asks looking sadly into Miss Veolia's solemn face.

"Chester? I guess he will come to live with me. I'm her only living kin since Mom passed on two winters ago."

He watches as the pair disappears around a corner onto Main Street.

"It is a sad thing indeed," he said under his breath.

"A tragic tale really!" said another voice from behind him. Miss Veolia has left but standing there looking down the road is Mr. Horne.

Lucio feels his hands begin to tremble slightly. He is noticeably uncomfortable now.

"A desert flower such as her, to be cut down in the prime of her life. It truly is unfair."

"Maybe it doesn't have to be that way," said Lucio with a twinge of anger in his voice.

"Come now, Lucio, 'gangrene', as Miss Veolia so eloquently tried to say, ends in a very, hmm, shall we just say 'uncomfortable finale'?" Gabriel stated.
Anger seems to overtake the nervousness in the troubadour as he stares into the suntanned face of Mr. Horne. He places his hand firmly on his guitar.

"Maybe we shall see a different ending this time, yes?"

"Lucio, let's drop the pretense" said Mr. Horne tugging at his cuffs of his suit coat He lingers on the left sleeve fidgeting with his forearm underneath then adjusts what appears to be a leather band around his index finger "I know who you are and I'm pretty sure you know who I am, am I right?"

Lucio clenches his teeth and stares out into the busy street. "Si" he said in a hushed but heated tenor. "I know who and what you are, señor. You have no place here today. This does not have to happen, no. What would her life or her death mean to one such as you?"

Mr. Horne draws in a Deep breath and smiles.

"Every life is precious, Lucio, you know that," he said with condescension. "But death is also a precious thing. How one chooses to come to final terms can mean a lot to any soul. Dignity and integrity regarding one's demise does tend to carry considerable weight in this place, Lucio. But life, life is always precious."

"Then maybe you are not here for Mrs. Weavers, no?" said Lucio with hope in his words.

Mr. Horne smirks. He reaches down and picks up the square case. The dapper dresser steps down into the street and places his white derby hat atop his head with a tap for good measure. He then turns back to Lucio.

"Alas, my dear Lucio" he said with a wink, "I think we both know why I'm here?"

CHAPTER 17

The town was in full bustle as Marshal Johnson stepped out from his office and onto Main Street. He looked into the rolling grey sky with disappointment as he began making his way south on the hectic thoroughfare. It looked like more rain again today he thought. His wrist again in agony, as he wrung his hands together,

Suddenly Lucio was at his side and appeared to be in a slightly agitated mood.

"Buenos tardes, Señor Johnson." he said in a hurried fashion.

"Well hola, Lucio. How are you?" he said noticing that the troubadour is intently rubbing his right wrist.

"I am good" Lucio replies in an obviously restless state.

"Something bothering you, Lucio?" asks Johnson.

"Si, I mean no, I mean . . . ," he stammers as his eyes scan the street frantically.

"Well which is it amigo, yes or no?" said the Marshal with a chuckle.

"I am looking for Señorita Weavers," he said in a huff, "I went by her casa but no one there. You know where she is?"

"Not for certain but if I was a betting man I'd say you'd catch her down at McMurphy's after all it's Saturday."

"Que, McMurphy's, señor?" asks Lucio.

"I'm sorry. McMurphy's General Store, its right over there on the corner of Second Street and Main across from the Grogan. It's Saturday so she and Chester are getting their weekly groceries."

Finally, a smile appears on his face.

"Oh Si, Si, señor! McMurphy's!" he said in an almost ecstatic manner while nodding his head quickly. "Gracias! Gracias!"

Johnson watches in amusement as the frenzied performer scatters away across the Main Street.

"Now what in Sam Hill was that about?" he said to himself with a grin.

Lucio gets to the front door of McMurphy's General Store just as LeAnn and Chester Weavers step out carrying a bundle of goods in both their arms. Lucio almost collides with LeAnn and this startles her to the point of dropping her bundle to the boardwalk with a dusty thud.

"Oh!" she shrieks.

"Lo Siento, señorita, I sorry!" said Lucio in a panic reaching down for the fallen sack of flour.

"Mr. Lucio, you startled me!" she said with a light laughter in her exasperated voice.

"I so sorry Señorita Weavers but I have been looking for you all afternoon" he said rapidly.

"Looking for me? Why?" she said fixing her hair from her face.

"Because I. . . " Lucio stops in mid-sentence as he sees LeAnn waving to someone across Main Street. He shifts his eyes to see whom and his eyes widen with fear. It is Mr. Horne and he is waving back. Lucio stiffens at the sight. Mr. Horne begins making his way towards them.

"No! Señorita LeAnn I must speak with you! Do not go towards him!" he said with alarm.

"Why? What's wrong?" she said with a puzzled look.

"I-I have a song for you! Si! Si! A song and you must hear it!" he said with a smile, his darting back and forth between her and the approaching Mr. Horne. "Could I sing for you now?"

Horne is now within a few feet of them.

"Oh my!" she suddenly cries raising a hand to her forehead. She starts to collapse but falls into Lucio's arms. He quickly moves her to a wooden bench on the boardwalk just to the right of McMurphy's entrance. He begins fanning her with his sombrero.

"Mom!" shouts Chester as he crouches beside her.
"Señorita! Señorita!" said Lucio with panic on his face. The store's owner, Larry McMurphy, seeing the event unfold through the big glass front window, rushes out the front door to offer his aid. He scoops LeAnn up in his long arms "Let's get her over to Doc's, I will carry her. Someone grab her groceries," he said in a take-charge fashion.

"Such a pity" said Gabriel Horne with indifference in his voice as he calmly watches the frantic proceedings. Lucio stares at Horne with terror-filled eyes as gathers her items. Then he, Larry McMurphy and Chester hastily make their way across Second Street and through the alley between Miss Veolia's and Grogan's Saloon and Dance Hall. Moments later, they emerge onto First St, just seconds away from Doc Johnson's door. They rush across the avenue and burst into Doc's office.

"Doc?" hollers Larry to no answer. "Doc!" he yells again!
LeAnn Weavers is still unresponsive as Larry McMurphy gently lays her on the leather covered examining table in Doc's parlor.

"No need to wake the dead for crying out loud!" came a voice from around the corner. Doc Johnsen stepped into the parlor fixing his eyeglasses around his ears. "Oh my word what's happened here?"

"The señorita, she fainted!" said a worried Lucio.

"What?" said Doc grabbing his black bag from the counter behind him?

"She was out front of my store when she just collapsed, Doc," said McMurphy.

"Fainted, eh?" said Doc.

"Si! Si! Fainted! Is she alright?" said the anxious troubadour.

"Well let me just have a look here first, huh?" said Doc with more than a twinge of sarcasm in his attitude.

He pulls out his stethoscope and begins listening to LeAnn's heart. His brow furrows a bit as he moves the device around LeAnn's chest. The tension in the room is palpable as they await Doc's diagnosis. Finally, Doc folds up the stethoscope and places it back in his black bag.

"Is she right-handed or left-handed?" Doc asks.

Lucio looks at Larry McMurphy in in confusion.

"She's right-handed," said young Chester from behind McMurphy.

"Why?" asks McMurphy.

"Just grab ahold of her right hand will you," he commands gruffly. "Get a tight grip on it too!"

"Alright I've got it," said the storeowner.

"Okay, here we go," said Doc. He begins lightly tapping the back of LeAnn's left hand. His brow furrows again. He taps it a little harder, again to no response.

"You sure you've got her hand?" he said glancing at McMurphy in the eyes with one of his own over his spectacles.

McMurphy nods in obvious confusion at the action. Doc then begins lightly tapping the left cheek of LeAnn's face. There is still no response. He taps a little harder now. Still no response.

Doc gives a very concerned look to McMurphy. A nervous Lucio leaves the room and steps out on the boardwalk. He looks up First Street towards Main Street, is

Gabriel Horne close. He wonders.

Sitting outside The Whiskey River is a brutish man in a chair leaning back against the wall of the saloon. The drunken man takes a long tug off of a half-filled bottle of tequila and spits most of it onto the boardwalk. The man then look over and sees Lucio. He raises the bottle up as if waving hello to the troubadour but Lucio turns his head away, partly in disgust, partly in concern for LeAnn Weavers' plight. Where is Horne, he must be near?

Lucio then slings his guitar from his back and plucks a few random strings as he sits down on the old wooden rocking chair that Doc frequently sit in. A tear trickles from the corner of his eye as the random plucking soon melts together into a single melody. He closes his eyes as if feeling each note with all his senses. Then softly he begins to sing:

> ♪She is a desert flower
> Both pretty and strong
> With a love big as Texas
> For her beloved son.
> She gives every minute
> Every hour, of the day
> To the boy she reveres.
> To the life that they make
> Yes LeAnn and Chester,
> Mother and son, not so old
> A bond they forged forever
> With the heart of gold.
> She'd gladly give her life
> to save her only son
> As I would my life
> For LeAnn's immortal soul…♪

As Lucio looks up, Gabriel is standing there across the road putting away his trumpet.

"Hey you, guitar player!" a gruff voice interrupts. Lucio opens his eyes to see the drunken man from the Whiskey Dollar now towering over him with an angry scowl on his face.

"What's the matter? You too good to speak with Milan Rodriquez?" the man said through clenched teeth.

Back inside the parlor, Doc Johnson gives a firm little slap to LeAnn's cheek, which again elicits no discernible response from the unconscious woman. He then looks up at McMurphy once more before then slapping LeAnn's face a bit harder.

Doc Johnsen is taken aback when this slap is reciprocated by an instinctive hard right hand slap to Doc's own face, courtesy of the now waking LeAnn Weavers.

"I thought you said you had ahold of her?" he barks at McMurphy.

"I didn't know how hard to grip her and I didn't want to hurt her," said Larry with a slight chuckle.

Doc rubs his cheek and glares at the shop owner.

"I'll remember that the next time you come in with the gout," he said with a determined nod.

Suddenly there is a loud crash from outside.

"See what in Sam Hill is going on out there, will you?" barks Doc at McMurphy.

Larry McMurphy nods and rushes out the front door onto the boardwalk. His eyes widen at the scene before him. There in the middle of the First Street is Lucio bleeding from his nose and mouth as he kneels in front of Milan Rodriquez. Lucio's shirt and hat lie in tatters in the dirt beside him revealing a badly scarred and marked body as in years of torture and brutality had been heaped upon his body. The group gasps at the sight of the wounds.

Lucio's guitar also lies in pieces, shattered by the hands

of the brutish outlaw. Rodriquez takes another healthy swallow from the bottle and kicks Lucio in the chest, sending the beaten man toppling backwards into the dirt in a cloud of dust. The skies overhead seem to darken as Rodriquez walks over and picks up Lucio by his curly brown hair.

"Chester ya gotta go and get Marshal Johnson!" said Larry McMurphy under his breath. The red haired boy disappears into the alleyway across from Doc's as Chester runs up the street.

"Do you not feel like singing for Milan Rodriquez, my friend?" asks the outlaw with a greasy smile.
"You, Sir would not like ugh, your song señor," said the trampled troubadour. "It has a very ugh, ah, a grim ending."
"Hah!" spits Rodriquez and shoves Lucio face first into the dirty street. Gabriel Horne was just about to intervene.

Marshal Johnson arrived quietly behind Rodriquez and stood next to Gabriel Horne.
Horne's alabaster eyes meet Johnson's and the two are locked in a momentary stare.
Marshal Johnson placing his gun against Rodriquez' back. "I should have kept you locked up!" said the Marshal, "On second thought, Judge Holmes is still on his annual fishing trip up north and won't be back for another week."
Marshal Johnson was now looking at Gabriel, "No sense in keeping you here, Gabe. I will file the paperwork. You're free to go, Mr. Horne."

Rodriquez reaches for his Colt, the Marshal fires first blasting a hole through his spine dropping him into the dirt street his blood pooling around his body. Doc Johnsen steps from his office and walks over to check the wound.

"Darn fool," said Marshal Johnson, "Doc there is no use in you checking on him he is not worth the time he has left if there is any?"

Doc Johnsen stands up saying, "He is dead, good thing he would just be paralyzed from that chunk of his spine lying over there anyway!"

"Lucio, calls LeAnn as she steps into the street, he is greeted with a hug by Chester and LeAnn Weavers. Doc Johnsen steps over to them and wraps a blanket around Lucio's shoulders.

"Come on, let's see if I can make you handsome again?" said Johnsen in his typical sarcastic manner.

As the pair walk up onto the boardwalk, Lucio glances back at Horne.
Horne winks and taps the top of his bowler hat.
Lucio smiles and now limping into Doc's parlor.

Inside the parlor, Doc hears a mordant horn playing a slow secular ballad. "I wonder what that is about?" he states.

Lucio smiles and rubs his bluing shin. "It is nothing to worry about now, señor?"

CHAPTER 18

Two days later, Lucio is sitting in a chair on the boardwalk outside the Overland Stage Office. He has his right foot and shin thickly bandaged and resting on a wooden crate. He is tuning a new guitar as he leans the chair back against the building. He softly strums a guitar, singing words barely audible by others.

♪"For storms will rage and thunders roar,
When Gabriel stands upon sea and shore,
When he blows upon his marvelous horn,
Old worlds die and new be born.
With the sound *of* ... Gabriel's horn."♪

"Quoting the Good Book now, are we?" asks a voice from inside the stage office.
"Si, señor" said Lucio. "I think it is only fitting, no?"

Gabriel Horne steps out onto the boardwalk. He is once again dressed in his white suit and matching bowler hat, square black and silver case firmly in hand, a slight smile on his face. He fidgets with the cuffs of his suitcoat.
"How's it sound?" asks the well-groomed Horne.
"She needs a little tuning, but she'll do," he said nodding as if resigned to the fact.
"Muchas gracias, to you sir."
"Yes, well, I'm sure you'll see to that!" assures Horne.

"And... You're welcome."

Both men look out into the busy street they see LeAnn Weavers playfully walking with her son Chester, her limping gait barely noticeable now. Lucio slowly gets up from his chair.

"Tell me, amigo, were you here for El Relampago the whole time?" asks Lucio.

Home chuckles slightly under his breath before answering.

"You should know better than to question... His will, my friend," he said straightening his bolo tie. "I see your foot is bandaged up. A souvenir from yesterday's unfortunate incident?"

"Si, I must have cut it on a broken bottle or something in the muddy street!" replies Lucio.

"Ah, yes, well make sure you take care of that nasty wound" he said matter-of-factly. "We wouldn't want you to get gangrene in it!"

Without looking at Horne, Lucio smirks a knowing smile.

"I'm glad to hear LeAnn Weavers' going to be with us for a long time," said Horne. "A boy needs his mother out here."

"Gracias, amigo." said Lucio looking up into Horne's eyes. Horne shrugs and stares out at the approaching stagecoach rumbling down Main Street, coming to a halt in front of the two men.

"We all have our role, Lucio," he said warmly and uncharacteristically and you truly are a saint."

"High praise from my angel of deliverance" retorts the troubadour.

Horne smiles.

"Where are you headed now, señor?" Lucio asked.

Gabriel Horne fidgets with the cuffs on his suitcoat.

"Not quite sure" he said. "I was thinking maybe north, Arizona perhaps. I hear there is a bit of business going on in a little mining town by the name of Tombstone. Perhaps I might be of some assistance there."

He then turns and offers his hand to Lucio who quickly grasps it. Shaking it firmly.

"Be well, my friend" said Horne as he steps down into the street into the stage.

"Vayu con Dios, amigo." said Lucio under his breath with a smile. "Vayu con Dios."

It is another typical morning in Steele Creek. The skies are once again grey with impending rain clouds, as is the norm here in the rainy season. Marshal Bode Johnson leans against a post outside his office and surveys the busy thoroughfare of Main Street This is where he feels he can get the pulse of his town. He sees the townspeople going about their very ordinary lives. Across the boulevard Mrs. Jansen, head matron of the Brazos Hotel, is beating the dust from a rug with a broom.

Just off to his right he notices Lucio, the troubadour, his foot wrapped tightly in medicinal cloth, as he shakes hands with the enigmatic aristocrat Mr. Gabriel Horne as the latter gets on the stagecoach in front of the Overland Stage Company. Still farther down the avenue, Larry McMurphy stocks the fruit into crates in front of his store.

The stagecoach rumbles by breaking the lawman's absentminded review. In the window, he sees Gabriel Horne. The pair exchange nods and soon the stage is obscured by clouds of dust. He looks up into the grey sky and shakes his head in disappointment at the prospect of more showers.

"Buenos Dias, señor!"

The words startle Bode Johnson gaze from the heavens back to earth. It is Lucio the troubadour, riding his mule, guitar firmly in hand.

"Well hola, Lucio," said Johnson. "You leaving us so soon?"

"Si señor," said Lucio with a wide boyish smile. "I have

many songs to sing and many to sing them to!"

Johnson laughs.

"Well you take care of that foot and come back to visit us, ya 'hear?" said the lawman pointing at the smiling Lucio.

One of the muddy cowboys had ridden in from the west and now stands nearby, he looks into the skies as rain begins to lightly fall.

Keenan Campbell the Gambler laughs.

"Even the angels weep for you, amigo" he said with arrogance.

"It is not for Lucio that they cry, bandito," said a coughing and groggy Lucio.

The words incense Keenan who stares down at Lucio with fire in his eyes. He throws the bottle of liquor to the ground, shattering it at the mule's feet. The impact jars Lucio's eyes open. He is now staring up the barrel of the outlaw's six-gun.

"I think I grow weary of your company, my friend and I hear the Marshal has shot my friend," hisses Keenan Campbell as he cocks the hammer back on his pistol.

"Since, it was over your rancid playing that I think maybe its time for you to sing now in the afterlife."

"Then I would gladly do so, señor, if it means adios to you" said a defiant Lucio.

"NO!" a woman screams. It is LeAnn Weavers. She stands in the doorway of Doc Johnsen's. The good doctor and her son stand beside her on the boardwalk.

Campbell turns his head sharply towards the trio. Suddenly a nasty smile creases his lips. Lucio squints through the drizzle and sees LeAnn standing there in horror. He manages weakened smile.

"Ah, there is an audience for your final performance, troubadour!" said Campbell with a laugh wiping the rain from his eyes. "Let's make it one that they will remember, eh mariachi? Maybe I should shoot them too!"

Suddenly the sound of loud hand clapping followed by a loud clap of thunder from the sky interrupts the proceedings.

"Well played! Bravo!" a calm voice said amidst the rain shower.

All eyes now shift to the figure walking down the center of the street towards the horrified group. Campbell wipes more rain from his brow and squints to see the man. The rain has become steadier and harder, making clear vision difficult for the outlaw and Lucio as well. The figure is dressed in a black suit. Campbell shields his eyes with his hands and can now see that there is something shiny in the figure's hand, and is held in front of his chest.

Lucio's eyes strained to see the man through the downpour. Then his eyes widened with dread.

"No, not Miss LeAnn." he said in exhausted breath too weak to shout.

The figure stops several feet from LeAnn and the others.

It is Gabriel Horne.

Against his chest, he holds a silver French horn.

"Perhaps you'd like me to play for you seeing as the troubadour's instrument seems to be . . . inaccessible?"

"Another musician?" grunts the outlaw. "Join the show, music man. I've got enough bullets for the whole band!"

Horne smiles and raises the horn to his lips. A loud yet heavenly note is heard. It is entrancing like a birdsong on a golden morning. As if on cue from the sound, the rain slowly stops. As the note continues to play the grey clouds above part, allowing a shaft of golden sunlight to stream down and act as a spotlight upon the immediate area.

The group gathered in front of Doc Johnsen's marveling at the scene unfolding. Campbell wipes the rain from his face with the sleeve of his grimy shirt. He glances up at the ray of sun peering down from the sky in confusion.

"Madre de Dios" said Lucio under his breath as he makes the sign of The Cross.

Gabriel ceases and lowers his instrument. He calmly places it safely onto the boardwalk.

"One note? That is all you play. Hah, I'll give you your reward after I finish business with the mariachi," growls Campbell.

"No, my friend, I believe your business is with me?" said Gabriel as he steps down into the street. He comes to a stop about ten feet from the outlaw and stands sideways near him, his left shoulder to the outlaw. Campbell cocks his head like a dog trying to understand some odd sound he has heard. He straightens back up and raises his pistol at the horn player.

"I'll kill you first then, it makes no difference the order of death," snarls Campbell.

"Yes well Death does have an order to It." said Horne matter-of-factly. He then raises his left arm and holds his hand out palm facing the outlaw. The bandit chuckles at the motion.

"You think to stop a bullet with your hand, horn player?" laughs Campbell.

"Not stop your bullet, but match it," said Horne calmly.
Campbell glances up and down the dark and dapper Horne.

"You're not even armed!" he spits.

"No? Oh my!" he said feigning alarm sarcastically. The tone angers the outlaw who levels the gun once more at Horne.

"Say goodbye horn player" said Campbell as he clenches his teeth and his finger tightens on the trigger.

Crack!

It happened in the blink of an eye.

Campbell's head snapped backwards then slowly forward. There was blood trickling from a hole in his forehead. He stood for a brief moment with a puzzled look on his face before falling to his knees and then face-first into the muddy street.

"Goodbye." Horne whispers.

In Gabriel Horne's left hand is a smoking small revolver, the kind that can be hidden up a sleeve on a sliding track and commanded into a hand at the tug of a line of twine around one's index finger. It all happened so fast that no one even saw the gun until it was over.

Horne walks over to the fallen Lucio and offers his hand. Lucio looks up at him with a bewildered look.

Things are not always as they appear, my friend," he said with a slight grin.

"Hold it Mister!" shouts Marshal Johnson walking up on the pair. Now noticing who it was. "How did you get here, I watched you leave by stagecoach."

"I fear I had no choice but to return to subdue this lout, Marshal," said Horne.

"I saw it," the lawman affirms. "It was self-defense alright but you'll still have to go before Judge Holmes."

"Alas, but I am again to be on the stage tomorrow for a return to the East," bemoans Horne.

Lucio laughs and strums his new guitar. He then rubs his right wrist as if it suddenly pains him. Then the Mexican minstrel waves heartily and begins strumming his guitar on, singing as he rides away down the boulevard.

♪He fought for justice and for God
A long life he would lead
For he was a man of true belief
Señor Johnson ... is ... indeed...♪

Johnson shakes his head in amusement at the sight. A drop of rain hits his cheek and he glances upward then back down at his right hand.

"Ain't that funny" he said.

Yes, Bode Johnson has always hated the rainy season but for the first time in years, he did not seem to mind it. Now noticing, his wrist did not hurt at all.

All that is left on stage is the echo of lingering memories from the performance just concluded. In a concert, if all of the musicians have played their parts right, the result a wonderfully melodious experience.

It is the same in life for a medley of circumstances in daily existence can build to a singularly momentous crescendo. While there are bound to be a few sour notes along the way, all would have to agree; it is better to have a song to sing than go through this world in silence.

Marshal Bode Johnson, Gabriel Horne, LeAnn Weavers, and Lucio.

They were the musicians in a production, which drew heavenly reviews. When the final note was played, the piece rendered seemed as if the Almighty Himself were its composer. Such an arrangement is what lures the imagination to the unimaginable, to a place where nothing is routine. Everyone has an important part in this earthly concert. It is the melody of living with the unknown and being ready for one's solo when the spotlight shines upon them.

No matter the role, angel or mortal soul, sinner or saint, each is welcome to take their place in the grand performance that is life.

Lucio is heard strumming as he rides away.

♪The music she has ended.

As curtain falls.

The band is now silent

As the audience exits the hall

Unspoken is the Grace of us all.♪

CHAPTER 19

Vengeance Must Prevail

Rodney Yates had seen Hagerty's younger half brother Keenan die in the street falling face first into the mud. Followed on by the group of ragged boys from town rummaging through his pockets, taking everything of value, from his rings on his fingers to his coat, pants and boots. The largest of the boys finished him by kicking Keenan in the mouth knocking loose his golden front teeth. The boy recovered them from the mud just as the undertaker arrived and chased the boys away.

They had just stolen half of his payment for preparing and burying his newest client.
"Damn, you street rats you just cleaned out this lout, cutting back on my profits, I sure wish the Marshal would run your little asses out of town, you homeless little bastards!"

Rodney Yates agreed the Bastards of Steele Creek must pay for this! He mounted his horse and rode out of town to the valley where Hagerty and the gang were holed up.

Yates explained what had happened to both Milan Rodriquez and his half-brother Keenan Campbell back in town. Maxwell Hagerty exploded with rage, threatening to seek revenge on the town as well as their original plans to rob the banks and saloons simultaneously.

Maxwell stomped around the camp kicking the small dog that had been following them, launching it up in the air and landing in the middle of the large bonfire. Burning the dog to death. The men all roared with laughter at the sights and sounds of the fires flare up and the dogs yelping in pain. Thankfully, for the small dog, that did not last long.

As the men gathered around the fire at dusk drinking whiskey from the bottles being passed around. Maxwell Hagerty stated, "We are going to move up the plan, tomorrow morning we shall ride in and wipe out the bank and saloon and any other building that may have stashes of money, we shall kill Marshal Johnson then we will burn the town, as we ride out for Mexico. Shoot to kill everyone in sight, men we shall leave there with no survivors!"

Another roar came from the gang as they swallowed more whiskey, passing the bottles around.

Steele Creek, Texas
That evening.

Marshal Bode Johnson, Sheriff John Hawk and Ranger James McCloud had been quietly preparing the towns folk for a week now and thought that they still had a few days before the gang's raid upon the town's bank and saloons.

Until a couple of the young boys that had stripped Campbell clean, had been talking in the O'Grady saloon, they were overheard telling about a man with muddy clothes, mumbling something about Maxwell's brother and riding hard out of town towards the valley. Bartender Ric Whalen hurried down the street to pass on what he had just heard to the Marshal.

Now with fear that the gang would move in sooner the Marshal, called out everyone to pass the word around town to get ready.

Prepare every man in town who could handle a gun and have the women organized to keep them supplied with cartridges or powder and shot. Soon all were gathered after dark, fortifying the Bank and Saloons front doors and had boarding over the windows. The stocks of supplies that had been kept in back rooms were now brought out and placed in positions to be at hand when needed.

By four a.m., the town was a fortress with barricades of overturned wagons and other large items blocking the streets and other items providing areas near the buildings where the town's shooters could use for cover and firing points. Every rooftop had at least five men hidden and at the ready with extra rifles and cartridges stocked up behind them.

Sheriff John Hawk had ridden out of town in the direction of the mountain valley to watch for any signs of the gangs approach. He passed the group of the town's men burying dynamite in rows as a pre-defensive measure.

Later he was sitting in a thicket of gooseberry bushes waiting. His horse 'Bo' had learned quite a bit from him and James McCloud about being alert and prepared for the unknown dangers of the rugged territories of the southern states. By wandering off further into the thicket to wait in safety, and not be seen by any one approaching.

Bo gave John his first clue of the gang approaching as he stopped grazing on the grass walking over to John and turned to face the west. Standing tall and not moving anything but his ears as they twisted and turned until the locked in on the distant sound of the approaching hoof beats, still to far off for Hawk to hear. Moments later John could see the dust rising over the horizon as the sun rose from the east.

Mounting Bo, Johnny galloped the horse back to town to alert everyone.

CHAPTER 20

Maxwell and the riders, now at least sixty men strong with the others that had joined them over the last week, were riding hard towards the east heading for Steele Creek unaware that the town was expecting them and had prepared for the attack. At five miles out of town, the riders spread out to attack with a larger front force and a follow-up force just shortly behind them.

At roughly one thousand yards from the town boarder, Cobb and Connelly pressed the two plungers down, some of the front riders were caught in the four explosions of 'TNT' placed out across their approach area. The explosions had only taken six men out and Maxwell felt he still had an upper hand and ordered another charge forward. The explosions had certainly slowed them up as the two men ran for cover they were shot down.

However, with Maxwell's orders to turn around and ride back, as he yelled for them to regroup and ride in again for another attempt. Maxwell was leading his men from the rear most position and far off to the north of the road leading in.

As the riders approached, again Ric Whalen detonated another row of three buried bundles of 'TNT' at least five of the horses with riders stumbled to the ground but this

time the riders remaining continued the charge. The rooftop riflemen started picking off the rider's one at a time with precise and single shots to their chests. They were falling from the horses hitting the ground hard as they died. Ric had made it to cover with the second barrage of rifle fire from McCloud and Hawk.
Those that continued riding ahead jumped their horses over the blockage in the street and shot at a few the town's men who had popped up their heads for return fire.

Once the riders were inside the perimeter of the town's outer defense. Several of the town's men dropped the cover wooden walls they had propped up and began firing a barrage of rifle fire into the center of the street, gunning down several more of the gang, some getting shot themselves and falling back through the now unprotected windows and doors of the shops and general stores. Behind the barricades remaining and inside buildings, the women and others began treating the wounds of those that were still alive at the time. Doc Johnsen was treating the wounded, as they were drug back to him in the rear of the Bank. Some of women replaced the men shot down and began shooting themselves protecting their town.

The battle of rifle, and small arms fire was beginning to fill the air with a grey-blue haze and the rotting egg smell of the gunpowder mixing with the coppery smell of the blood pooling around the bodies scattered around the street and boardwalks.

When the gang had been reduced to less than a dozen men. Some began to hightail it out of town, Maxwell shot a few of his own men riding away killing them in the retreat. Marshal Bode Johnson shot at Maxwell Hagerty putting a round of lead that passed through his thigh killing his horse.

Maxwell crawled in behind one of the overturned

wagons and began returning fire from this new position of cover.

The remaining gang inside the town soon joined him behind the wagon, taking cover there as their horses ran off.

The wagon provided them great cover as it had furniture and pianos from the saloons making a small circle of protection around them.

Several more of the town's men and women were killed in the exchange of fire, as the wagon and pianos was too great a cover for the eight men inside the circle. They continued to pick off the unexperienced at shooting men and women of Steele Creek.

At the end of the street walking in the open dead center of the street was the man who had a second time left town on a stage, had returned it was Gabriel Samuel Horne.

The man was dressed again in his white suit, dark blue shirt and white bolo tie with a silver conch and turquoise stone in the center. He was clean-shaven and immaculately groomed. In his visible hand was a silver trumpet held tight to his chest.

Maxwell and his men began firing at him as he approached, Bode and McCloud yelled at him to get out of the street but he continued to walk forward towards the wagon and the men shooting at him. McCloud could see the bullets hitting him in the chest and upper thighs the blood spurting from his wounds, but he continued walking ahead.

At three yards from the wagon, he swung his hidden arm around from behind his back and threw a triple stick bundle of dynamite with what was now a very short fuse over the piano into the center of the circle. It exploded just as it passed over the top of the piano in midair.

The noise and flash was horrendous as the entire center

of the street and barricades splintered and disappeared in a
ball of fire and large black mushroom cloud.
Gabriel Samuel Horne was consumed inside the blast.

All firing ceased as some of the town's folk still alive
climbed out from behind the cover and stood watching the
debris falling back down creating small fires as it reached
the old wooden structures. They began fighting down the
fires and soon had all under control.

Bode, James and John along with a few others searched
around in the rubble finding Maxwell and seven other
bodies or body parts and stacked them on the north side
boardwalk of the main street. No one could identify in any
of the remains the body of Gabriel Horne in the debris or
of the body parts lying on the street and boardwalk.

By the end of the day, the gang members had been
gathered from where they fell, stacked on a large grain
wagon and pulled outside of town to the nearby valley that
they had used for camp prior to the attack. Here the
wagon was doused in lantern fuel and set ablaze.

An entire week past with the cleaning up of the town
before they held the funerals of the town's folk who died.
Each one held separately to honor that person buried in
his or her grave.
At a special place in the Cemetery was placed a wooden
tombstone marked Gabriel Samuel Horne, with the
reading below the name.

'Music, when soft voices die, the tune vibrates the memory.'

Sheriff John Hawk and Texas Ranger stayed for the
funerals before riding out for Dallas and Nogales.
Before leaving town ranger McCloud explained to
Bode that the warrant for him had been pardoned by the

Governor, and that he was there to find out if Bode had really turned his life around.

Holding out his hand, he said, "Mr. Bode Johnson I am proud to say that you have done just that, Sir."

On the second night at the campsite they prepared for the night, both of their horses began lightly stomping, waking them up to what might be danger approaching. As they arose and took protective cover with pistols and rifles at the ready. The dark moon and thick fog made it extremely dark and hard to see very far from camp side.

Moments later a man on horseback quietly rode past now close enough to see from the fire light.

The man was dressed in his white suit, dark blue shirt and white bolo tie with a silver conch and turquoise stone in the center, siting straight and tall riding a large white stallion.

James and John watched him until he was again out of site into the darkness, splitting the fog and trotting away from Steele Creek a solemn trumpets note reverberating into the night.

Shaking his head McCloud simply said, "I hope we are dreaming!" and laid back down on his blanket tucking his Henry rifle in close by his side.

Johnny Hawk sat up the remaining of the night, with his rifle on his lap.

CHAPTER 21

Shortly before the sun rose the next morning, James arose to the smell of bacon and corncakes over an open fire. John Hawk had not slept much overnight at what they thought for sure they had seen, neither had been asleep dreaming, as it was as real as real could get.

In the early hours before James awoke John had attended to the animals cleaned up around the camp and had started breakfast. Noticing James stirring he called out to him, "Hey Ranger it is a glorious new day the air is crisp and I am just about finished with the cooking you might want to shake it loose and get up."

James sat up on his bedroll and stretched again the aroma of the clean mountain air, cooking food and fresh coffee blended into a wonderful medley James so loved about the wilderness of Texas.

"I bet that the gambler that called you my servant would love to know that he was pretty close to being right!" said James laughing.

"Like you said then, I am not your servant just a good friend. Anyway, I awoke early so I decided to make good use of my time and get things started." James wandered off into the trees to relieve himself and returned grabbing a tin cup and filling it with the coffee hammering back a jolt of the bitter liquid. "Damn John that is good, real hot and strong just as I like it?"

"Well sit on down and try some of these corncakes and bacon slabs, before you go bragging about my cooking!"

James looked as he was about to wander out towards the trail, when John spoke up, "Don't bother to check, I have already taken a look over there and yes, there is a single set of fresh tracks from a rider that passed by here last night and like we said then. We were not dreaming he did passed by this way sounding that trumpet as he rode on!"

"Tracks really, well he rode on and caused no harm and by the looks of your bedroll you did not sleep at all last night?"

"Okay so it kept me awake, now get on over here and try some of this before I totally burn it all!"

James sat on one of the logs they had used the night before as his chair and served himself a large helping of the food remaining in the skillet.

"Well to tell the truth I did not sleep too soundly after that either. I kept waking up hearing you're rustling around and keeping out a good watch, so I just stayed covered up and grabbed a few winks here and there. We most likely will have a quiet ride ahead of us so as long as you do not fall from your saddle you can grab a few winks as we ride."

It was not long into the morning ride when Johnny dozed off and let Bo's steady gait follow McCloud along the trail. It was getting close to two in the afternoon when John sat up complaining about his stiff neck and back from slumping over along the ride. They pulled in and headed over near a row of trees to rest the horses and get some blood flowing again in the shade. The first thing John did after dismounting Bo and letting him wander off to find some prairie grass to nibble on, he laid down on the ground near a tree and stretched out straight. James opened a couple cans of beans with his knife and handed one to John. "There you go now were even, I fixed us lunch." John sat up groaning at his stiff back as he took the can from James and dug a silver spoon out from his satchel, he had pulled from the saddlebags before Bo had walked off.

"Thanks for letting me sleep, I should have followed you and just laid down last night, the rider sure had me spooked."

"It was most likely someone from town dressed up just trying to play a game and see if they could rattle us some. Let's not worry about it now."

"Probably so, probably so! Well let's share a little water with the horses and move on."

They rode on in silence most likely both were thinking about the rider last night and had not thought about making conversation. It was nearing late afternoon most likely three to four p.m. when McCloud's horse stopped dead in his tracks not moving a muscle, Bo quickly caught on and followed suit. Both men sat stoically in the saddles as four handkerchief masked men stepped out from the trees with their pistols in hands, pointing at them.

"Hold up your hands, both of you!" one of the men growled.

James sized up the situation as the men spread out across the road in front of them. John had turned his head to see if there was anyone behind them to his relief there was no one in sight.

"Okay we have you covered so just ease them there weapons out and toss them on the ground."

"Do it now!" a second man demanded.

James thumbed the strap from his colt and with just two fingers started lifting it from his holster. John followed along pulling his and they dropped them in the dirt next to the horses.

"Okay now ease out those rifles and toss them aside."

James un-fastened the strap of his saddle scabbard and lifted his Henry out slowly, he shifted the rifle to his other hand and leaned sideways over Argo, intending to place it on the ground. At the same time, Argo spread his front legs trying to balance the shifting weight of his rider. James was now slightly blocked from view as he gently lifted his razor-sharp Bowie knife from the sheath inside his boot. John had been moving a bit slower removing his Henry as two of the men stepped up closer pointing there guns at John and James.

James heard what he was expecting; the sound of the hammers on the pistols being pulled back, he was not surprised that they did not plan on leaving any witnesses to the robbery.

In one quick motion, Argo raised his head and bumped the man in front of him hard in the chest knocking him backwards onto his Ass. James straightened in the saddle firing the rifle and whipping the knife with the other hand. The bullet had hit its target hitting the man who demanded they hold up their hands, the knife scored less than a second later in another mans chest.

John had taken aim on the third man and fired one round into his forehead leaving a small entrance hole and removing the back of his skull on exit, knocking him backwards several feet. The two men James had taken out stood for a moment before it registered to the rest of their bodies that they were already dead, dropping straight to the ground. The forth man was attempting to get up when Argo kicked him on his head knocking him backwards again. James was down flat on the ground looking for others that may have been in waiting. John then rolled the forth man over and tied his hands together behind him.

On their feet now, the lawmen stood over the one still alive and rolled him over with their boots. He was roughly fifteen years old, and looking at the others, none could have been over twenty.

John began scolding the boy, "What in the hell were you thinking, you stupid bastard. Three of you are dead and you are going to jail with us and will probably hang for attempting to rob and kill two Law Enforcement Officers."

"We were not going to kill you we just wanted your money and horses?" he cried out.

"Okay so you have just admitted to armed robbery and horse theft, which will still get you Life in prison most likely." McCloud said adding, "Sheriff John Hawk here is from Nogales not to far from here, and I am a Texas Ranger from the Dallas Office for this territory."

The boy was now sobbing almost out of control as they stood over him. It was nearly ten minutes before he regained control of himself. John helped him to his feet noticing that he had wet his pants. John did not say anything about it as he spoke to the boy, "Just as Ranger McCloud said we are not far from Nogales, so you can walk on ahead of us and we should be there in a few hours. From here to there, it will be open desert prairie so you have no need to try and run from us. You'll just tire yourself out."

James handed him a canteen after untying his hands and pointing down the trail towards Nogales. "Just follow the trail and we will arrive in town as soon as you make the walk?"

They stopped several times along the way for the boy to rest, and by the third stop he had regained his stubborn courage and began back talking them as they rode on. "You have room on those horses, one of you could let me ride?" he said.

"Well that might be true but the four of you had made

it out this far without on foot, so we are sure you alone could make it back." John said.

"And you just left them out there, dead they were my friends?"

"We will send a wagon out to pick up what the coyotes don't drag away. You can let us know their names later in town."

"You can just piss up a rope. I am not going to tell you anything!" he growled.

James spoke this time, "Well maybe you could've pissed up the rope instead of in your pants, boy!"

"I am not a boy, I am fourteen and old enough to be on my own!"

"Maybe so, maybe so, just keep on moving down the trail!" John said.

They arrived at John's office at around Two a.m. the boy barely dragging his feet along, they were met by one of John's deputies. He had just returned from his rounds and had taken a seat in the old rocking chair on the boardwalk.

"Welcome back Sheriff, and to you too Ranger McCloud, who is this you have here?

"Thanks Brice, he would not give us his name or the name of his three accomplices' they are back about ten to fifteen miles along the trail."

"On the trail?" he asked.

"Yep, tried to rob us and take our horses, most likely would have killed us too! If they had been smarter or quicker. Get Robby up and have him take one of his wagons out there and bring back the bodies for identification. They will be along that bend in the road where the tree line starts."

"Three of them, I'll let him know to take help with him?"

STEELE CREEK

It was after five a.m. before Robby and Gus returned with the wagon and their cargo. Deputy Brice Logan was still at the office, having had the night shift this week.

"Take them on down to the undertaker and have him clean up what is left of them, either of you recognize them?"

"The longest one wrapped up is Eric Blair the other two are Stevie Jensen and his brother Stanley. Most likely we figure you have Jimmie Harris inside locked up, since they are always running together!" said Robby.

"Okay the Sheriff and Ranger McCloud will be in after they are up and had breakfast. I will let them know, 'suppose they will have some notifications to make later. So keep this between just the three of us okay."

"We know the drill, Brice. That is why you count on us to do the dirty work." Gus said laughing.

Sheriff, John Hawk and Ranger McCloud rode out to the Jenson Ranch passing under the Double V sign suspended between to tall poles on each side of the road leading up to the Jenson's home. Two dogs welcomed them with enough barking that Mr. Jensen was out on his front steps when the pulled up to the rail. They tipped their hat to him before they dismounted and tied off the horses.

Stanley Jensen greeted them asking why they were out his way. John introduced Ranger McCloud then broke the news as gently as he could to the portly man. Stanley senior grabbed the handrail and seated himself on the steps, saying. "Well at least their Mother will not have to hear this," he said through the tears welling in his eyes, "she passed on three weeks ago from the consumption!"

"We are so sorry to hear that, Mr. Jensen. You will be able to make arraignments in town with the undertaker he will prepare the bodies and the wooden caskets for you."

replied McCloud.

"We have to move along and if you have questions later you're welcome to stop by my office for a copy of the reports." John said.

Together they rode on to the Blair's place.
Upon arrival at the small ranch, house Mrs. Blair was tending to her small garden and Mr. Blair was out in the field behind two of his old horses plowing up some of the field.

Sheriff John Hawk dismounted as James rode out across the field to bring Mr. Blair up to the house.

Mr. Blair insisted on knowing why they were there before he would quit working. James told him what had happened and that there had been no choice but to defend themselves. Larry Blair charged James like a bull hearing the news of his sixteen-year-old son's death by gunfire from the Ranger. James sidestepped the man who was at a full run, pushing him to the ground. Larry was back on his feet and ready for another attempt when James spoke loudly.

"Knock it off Mr. Blair, I do not want to harm you, you need to go to the house and comfort your son's Mother." That was enough to make him stop as he dropped to his knees sobbing. Moments later, he stood and walked towards the house.

James remounted Argo and slowly walked him alongside the distraught man.

Once inside the Sheriff told them where they could recover their son and if they wanted a copy of the reports.

Eight days had passed before the Judge making his rounds along the Judicial, circuit made it to Nogales. The trial was heard and Jimmie Harris was given his chance to tell his side of the story.

The eight days in jail had him stoic and he began.

"Stanley and Stevie made the plan and talked me and Eric into going along on it."

"That should be Stanley, Stevie Eric and I" said Judge Holmes."

"That is what I said, the brothers talked us into it and we went along, me and Eric!"

The crowd laughed at his attempt of English, as Jimmie continued confused by the laughter. "Well we din't count on it bein' the Sheriff and a Texas Ranger we robs, so they all got kilt and the Rangers horse attacked me or I'd be just as kilt as the others." The crowd began laughing again, Judge Holmes used the butt of his gun as a hammer on the desk and told them to be quiet or he would clear the courtroom.

"Jim Harris do you have any Family in this area?" the Judge asked.

"Nope, jus me. My parents were kilt when they rollt' our wagon over in the rivar. I was ten whenst that happened and I rided one of the mules we had to here and sold him. Whenst I runned out of that money I just did what ever I could to survive, stealing n' stuff. That is when I met Eric."

"Okay, we have heard enough, and by your admittance of the armed robbery and attempted murder of two of our finest law enforcement officers. Also, with your obvious lack of any education. I have no other choice then to sentence you to the State Penitentiary for no less than Forty Years."

"Forty years, thats awfully long time juge!"

"Yes it is, Deputy see to it that the next prison wagon picks up Mr. Harris here, until then he will remain in your custody here in Nogales!" he hammered his pistol again on the desk and stood to leave. Thank you all. Court is adjourned.

Judge Harris met McCloud and Hawk at the Lemoine River Saloon, where they were waiting for him with a bottle of Whiskey.

"I hear that you two have a story to tell about a visionary. A ghost rider if that is how you want to describe it along the trail ride here, would you mind sharing the story with me?"

James McCloud began laughing as John's face turned a bright red.

"I would rather we did not bring that up again, how in the hell did you hear about that?" asked Johnnie Hawk.

"Oh, no never mind, the word just seemed to get around somehow!" Harris replied.

James said, "No don't look at me Johnnie, I am surprised as you are to hear that it is being talked about!" Sheriff John Hawk took a long pull straight from the bottle, and remained quiet.

James rode out for Dallas, the next morning following breakfast with Judge Holmes and Sheriff John Hawk.

CHAPTER 22

The afternoon sun reflecting off the coat of the dappled gray horse made him glisten as if he was wearing a blanket of shiny pearls. He galloped across the sandy desert with his long white mane and tail floating in the wind. The man on his back wore a black Stetson hat and duster, which flowed onto his mount's flanks and made the two look fused together. Horse and rider loped along the gritty dirt through the sagebrush until they arrived at the banks of a river. The rider urged the horse to wade into the swiftly flowing river and the water slowly wrapped around its slate black legs until it touched the stirrups of the saddle as they made their way to the other side.

The trees along the sides of the river were green and leafy and the vegetation at the water's edge was thick and lush. Through the wispy branches, the horse took notice of a coyote nervously sniffing the ground and the horse immediately became wary.

The horse's attentiveness to the coyote alarmed his rider and he pulled his mount's head around and cautiously guided him out of the water to the side of the trail where he brought the horse to a halt. He waited there to see if he could spot what the horse and coyote were worried about but when the coyote saw the man on top of the horse it took off, man is a much bigger threat than anything else found in the wilderness.

As the man looked around trying to see what might

have startled the creature a large silvery grey wolf came trotting out of the brush and ran up to the duo. The horse acknowledged the animal's presence with a snort but still cautiously gazed about. Something had spooked both the horse and the coyote and it was not likely that it had been the wolf. A lone wolf rarely attacks anything other than a rabbit and never a coyote and the horse already knew the wolf.

Jonas got off his horse, crouched down and peered through some scrub trees as he surveyed the area ahead. As soon as he hit the ground, the wolf approached him.

"Are you out here causing trouble Cody?" The tail wagged as the animal came up for a pet. When the man stood up his black duster spread out around him like a cape and spooked the creature.

"Really? What's got the two of you so jumpy?" Jonas said as he got back on the horse and pressed it to a gallop along the river with the wolf following close behind.

They followed the bend in the trail ahead and soon entered a shabby looking town. It was composed of several crudely built structures, some looked like houses, some like temporary shelters and the large permanent appearing building had several horses tied up in front with a sign that had Whiskey and Beer carved onto it. Jonas rode up to the saloon stopping his horse, dismounted and threw the reins over the hitching post.

"Stay here." He told the silver shadow that had immediately lain at the horse's feet after he got off. Jonas Lawrence confidently walked through the door and strode up to the bar. The patrons stared at him; probably because he wore his gun strapped to his leg like a gunfighter but also because he was a stranger.

Jonas was a good six-foot tall, sinewy with dark black hair and dangerous flashing black eyes and strong good looking features. He wore a tanned elk hide shirt. He quickly gazed around the room registering the glances of the men and women, which made him cautious. None of them seemed to be able to take their eyes off of him. He knew he had not been in this odd little place before so he was wary as to the attention he was receiving.

He had been in a lot of small towns, and he remembered them all and many were quite similar to this one. Most of them had a store, a Doctor's office, a saloon, and a few houses for the important people and assorted lodging for everyone else. The larger towns usually had a bank, a church and some kind of law office but lately they were mostly small settlements like this than like the larger ones in the territories, he had been traveling through they were all mostly, lawless.

Behind the bar, the old man sized him up as he walked to the counter. The bartender's grizzled appearance was in stark contrast to Jonas. His skin was taut, weathered and wrinkled, his hair was grey and his beard was white whereas the stranger was sleek, dark and moved with the grace and danger of a mountain lion. The bartender was strong and sturdy and had no problem keeping the young cowhands in line but he had seen many more years pass by than the man had now standing there had.

"Give me a whiskey please." Jonas politely asked.

"Sure thing, I haven't seen you in here before." He was trying to gauge the young man's attitude.

"That's true." Jonas tersely replied.

"What's your name, stranger?" The bartender inquired.

"Do you need my name before I can get a drink?" Jonas quipped.

"No sir, I don't. Settle down now." He was not trying to rile the man up.

"I am settled, how about less talking and more drinking. My name's Jonas." He responded with a hint of a smile tugging at the corners of his mouth. "Why's everyone staring at me?"

"Don't mind them, you're new in town and there's nothing much to do round here. People here call me

Boss." The old man said as he felt at ease around this stranger.

Jonas drank his whiskey and watched the men sitting at the corner table playing cards out of the corner of his eye. They nervously glanced over at him and whispered to each other. He could hear pieces of their conversations.

"Isn't that the man that killed old Pete Wilson in Tucson last month?"

"It sure looks like him."

"He shot Pete before he even got a hand his gun out of the holster."

Jonas ignored the gossip and finished his drink just as a cocky young man walked up to the bar.

"Can I buy you a drink?" The young man asked.

"No thanks." Jonas answered.

"Are you too good to have a drink with me?" The young man became agitated.

"No, I just had one but if you're gonna cause trouble you can buy me another." Jonas quietly remarked.

The bartender cautiously approached the two men, and poured a couple shots of whiskey and set them on the counter.

"I knew he wouldn't pass up a free drink." The young man smiled as he made this announcement to the saloon. Everyone nervously watched the two men.

"I let you buy me a drink so how about you quit talking?" Jonas was getting annoyed.

"What do you mean by that?"

"Nothing but what I just said. I am minding my own business so why don't you do the same?" Just as Jonas spoke the young man reached for his gun and a second later, he was lying on the floor with a bullet in his leg. The young man cried out in pain and cursed Jonas. Comments quickly came from the men sitting around the saloon.

"It was a fair fight mister. He drew first." Numerous

men quickly chimed in their affirmation.

Jonas looked around. "Alright then everyone stay where you are and I'm gonna leave. I had to shoot after he pulled his gun on me but he won't die from his wound." Jonas put money on the bar for his whiskey and carefully walked out of the saloon watching the men while he did.

Jonas mounted his horse and quickly rode out of town watching behind him for the men he was sure that would follow. He rode to a nearby stand of trees next to a large outcropping of rocks by a watering hole after he was clear of the town. He got off and motioned to the wolf to take off and he tied his horse to a tree behind the rocks. He found a location on top that provided cover and waited for the men to come after him.

It was not long before four men arrived; they dismounted and allowed their horses to drink water while they studied the ground to determine which way the man they were tracking had gone. As they studied the recent tracks, when they heard the sound of a gun being cocked. They looked up and saw Jonas standing on the rocks overhead holding a rifle on the man leading the group. That man was big, burly and looked like a lawman.

"Put up your hands and drop your guns unless any of you think I can miss at this distance?" Jonas fiercely stared at all of the men and kept his gun focused on the leader of the bunch. The men slowly dropped their weapons to the ground.

"So what do we do now Hank?" A skinny nervous man wearing a tacky leather fringed jacket addressed their leader. Before he could answer, Jonas did.

"If I were any of you I would get on my horse and ride out of here. You only have a couple of minutes to decide what you are going to do before I start shooting. It's your choice which way this goes down." Jonas kept his gun steadily trained on its original target as the men all pulled their horses heads away from the water and mounted up.

Jonas called out, "If this little posse came after me because of the man I just shot you ought to go back and ask what really happened. It was a fair fight that, I could not avoid. He drew first and I only shot him in the leg to keep either one of us from getting killed."

Just then, a man at the back of the pack went for his hidden boot gun, Jonas quickly shot it out of his hand and just as fast, his Colt was retrained on the leader.

"Okay, we get the message. We're gonna leave." Hank said and the men turned their horses around and galloped off.

Jonas waited until the men were out of sight and picked up their guns. He retrieved his horse from where he tied it and then headed in the opposite direction at a rapid pace. He did not think the men were going to come back without their guns but he saw no reason to take any chances since they probably were going to come back and get their guns eventually. No man likes to lose his gun.

"Whoa Diablo" Jonas halted the horse after a bit in the middle of the trail.

He took the bullets out of the guns putting them in his saddlebag and then tossed the empty guns out onto the dirt. If they did come back they could not accuse him of stealing their guns but they could not shoot him either.

The late afternoon sun was blazing hot and he was looking for a place to escape from the heat when he noticed a wagon up ahead on the horizon. He approached it cautiously and saw that the wagon was being hauled by four mules with two handsome sorrel horses tied to the back. As he got closer, he could see a husky looking young man manning the reins with a beautiful woman sitting by his side and on the tail end of the wagon sat a teenage boy. The wagon was sagging low on its axles seemingly carrying a heavy load. He followed behind them for a bit. Jonas saw an even odder collection of structures coming up than the last little settlement he was in. When he got closer he could see several horses tied up in front of the largest building just like at the previous location. The wagon arrived there first and stopped in front. There was a sign hanging out front which said 'Whiskey Stop.' The saloons were by far the biggest and most popular places in any town he ran across no matter what the size.

While the man with the wagon was tying up the mules and gathering his family together Jonas left his horse, with the wolf guarding it, beside the saloon. He walked around front to the batwing doors and entered. There were five men sitting around a table drinking whiskey and playing cards and another wearing a black vest standing next to the bar.

"Howdy there stranger, what can I do you for?" The man with the black leather vest asked while obviously sizing him up.

"I'm thirsty, hungry and lookin' for a place to get some food and water for me and my horse." Jonas answered.

"You come to the right place. There's a man at the stable next door that will feed and water your horse for two bits while you eat here." The man with the vest replied.

"That's what I'm lookin' for." Jonas said but before he could say more the family came walking in from the wagon. The men looked up from their game and stared at the very attractive woman, with a boy standing behind her.

"Can you tell me if there's a place to buy supplies around here?" The man asked the man at the bar.

"Don't you and your misses want to order a drink first?"

The man looked at the bartender and answered.

"Umm, sure. Water, we'll pay for it." The man nervously replied.

"I don't serve water here. I got beer and whiskey." The

man poured two whiskies and a beer set them on the counter. "What brings you to Whiskey Stop?"

"We're looking to buy some supplies and spend the night where we don't have to worry about getting attacked by Indians." The man nervously responded as he gave the beer to the boy and motioned to the woman to take one of the whiskies.

The men in the bar gazed lustfully at the beautiful woman as she took the shot of whiskey and drank it.

"You can camp next to town tonight. There's a place across from this here saloon that stocks some supplies." The barman said as he looked out past the swinging doors at the fancy horses tied to the wagon.

"Thanks. How much do I owe you?" The man wanted to get out of there fast. The way the men were looking at the woman was making him nervous.

Just then, the man behind the bar turned his attention back to Jonas. "This is turning out to be a right busy day here. What did you say you wanted?"

"I didn't. I'd like whiskey and water." Said Jonas he was thirsty after riding all day.

"We don't serve water here didn't you hear?"

"Then I guess you better give me whiskey and beer." Jonas was not surprised but he wanted to see if he got the same treatment as the family did.

As the man got Jonas' drinks, the other man put money on the bar and quickly left with the woman and boy.

Jonas drank the whisky swiftly and then slowly drank the beer. He savored the sensation as it flowed down his throat it was refreshing. He paid up and went to get his horse fed and watered. He was ready to leave this strange little settlement by now. The men seemed treacherous and he had already dealt with enough of that for one day. Getting his horse cared for was the only important thing he needed to do.

The family was still standing in front when Jonas walked out from the saloon. "Howdy folks." He greeted them.

The young man looked at Jonas and deduced he was not a threat. "Hi stranger, kind of an odd little place here isn't it?"

"Yeah I suppose it is. There are lots of places like this out here. Where are you folks headin' to?" Jonas replied.

"A place called Los Angeles, California. We came out from Virginia but we parted company with the wagons we were traveling with after some of the families got sick. We decided it was best if we headed out on our own. Now I'm not so sure it was such a good idea." He looked distressed.

"I know what you mean but most of those men are harmless. You do have a fine looking wife, and son. My name's Jonas Lawrence." He was looking at the woman as he addressed the young man.

"I'm Jake this is my sister Anna and her son Jesse. Anna's husband died in an accident on the trail about a month ago." His response was sad but friendly.

"Sorry to hear that. I'm headed to California also and then on down to Mexico."

"We're going to get some supplies and camp near here tonight and then head out in the morning. Would you like to join us for dinner?" Jake inquired.

"That's a mighty fine offer and I haven't had a good meal in a long time. I have been living on jerky, biscuits and venison. I'm gonna see about getting my horse fed right now but I'd be right pleased to have dinner with you folks." Jonas responded.

"I thought we should stay next to this little town tonight because I knew we were entering Indian Territory. I wanted to sleep where we didn't have to worry about getting attacked but those men in the saloon look more dangerous than any of the Indians I've seen." Jake commented.

"I saw the way they were lookin' at your sister but the Indians I've met are kind of like rattlesnakes, if you don't bother them they won't bother you. The men in this town remind me of vultures, just waiting around to prey on the sick and the weak. With me and you around I don't think they'll bother us any." Jonas looked at Anna when he responded.

"I'd sure appreciate your help. You look a lot more capable than I do. I know I'm not much of a gunfighter and so does everyone else." Jake looked at his sister and her son when he said this.

"That's nothing to be ashamed of. I'll come by your camp after I get my horse taken care of." Jonas turned and walked off.

Jonas and the family went about their business. He took his horse and saw the man at the stable. "For two bits I'll feed, water and brush down your horse and if you want you can leave him here overnight." The old man told him.

"I don't need that, I'll be back to get him in a couple of hours. I'm gonna leave my dog here with my horse but he won't bother you if you don't bother him."

"Your dog? He looks more like a large wolf!"
Jonas sensed the man's nervousness but he did not care. The wolf and the horse were both safer if they stayed there together.

The man looked at the wolf with suspicion but did not object. Jonas thought the men in this town seemed shady just like Jake had. He went to the building that sold supplies and bought a few things for himself along with some bacon and eggs to give to the family he had been invited to have dinner with, secretly hoping to be invited to breakfast the next morning. He still had some meat left in his saddlebags from the deer he killed for him and Cody as well as some flour, salt, sourdough and some beans.

While he was waiting for his horse to be cared for he went back to the saloon for a few more shots of whiskey and beers. He got a few odd looks from the men still playing cards but they left him alone and that suited him just fine. The man in the black vest was still standing there also. "Back so soon, sir!" he had asked.

Jonas took, another look at him wondering why this man seemed so inquisitive. "I have my horse being tended to down at the stable and decided to wait here and have another drink, if that is okay with you?"

"Sorry I did not mean anything about it, Just trying to make conversation, that's all." He said, By the way my name is James McCloud."

"Nice to meet you James, I am known as Jonas Lawrence." As he held out his hand to shake. James responded saying, "I am just heading back up towards Dallas would you be riding that way?"

"No my plans are heading west to California and then on south into Mexico."

They grabbed a nearby table and continued talking more. The others playing cards watched them for a moment then went back to their card game.

McCloud had learned that Lawrence was just wandering the new territory before deciding to settle down. Jonas finally asked James about his life and plans.

"Actually I am a Texas Ranger from the Dallas Regional Office and had rode to the far southern end near Brownsville to a small town called Steele Creek."

I have heard of that town, I remember reading about a new Marshal down there and how he has turned the town around. In addition, there was a story about the Maxwell gang being beaten down by the Marshal and the town's folk working together. You wouldn't have had something to do with that now would you?"

"I was there but the story is right the Marshal is a good man and rallied the town into protecting themselves against the raid. I would say he did a mighty fine job too!"

Soon they both headed for the stables to retrieve their horses. McCloud was well known for being able to tell a man's character just by speaking and observing him. James said he would ride on through the night before finding a place to stay the next evening.

This man Jonas Lawrence was just that, a good and

honest man, he knew he would take good care of the family. Parting their ways James rode on out of town.

Jonas retrieved his horse and went to find the family. They were set up just outside of the makeshift town in the westerly direction they were all headed. Jonas had been traveling for a long time, he was starting to miss the home and family he left behind. He was looking forward to good food and decent company.

Anna was tending the fire when Jonas walked into camp. She was a beautiful woman and he could not help but stare at her. She had a nice figure, and her face was beautiful and her golden hair was tied neatly up on her head.

"Howdy mam, where's Jake and Jesse?"

"They're out gathering more wood for the fire." She pointed behind the wagon. "What's that following you?"

"That's Cody. He and my horse, Diablo, have been on the trail with me for a long time." Jonas answered.

"He looks like a wolf." She looked a bit concerned.

"That he is. I came across his mother dead in a trap when he was just a pup and I saved him and he has been with me ever since. He watches over my stuff and helps me hunt deer. Diablo and Cody are my friends and we all watch out for each other." He watched her to see if she thought he was crazy. Most people did not call animals' friends but she did not react to his statement.

"What part of the country did you come from?" She changed the subject.

"I grew up in New Mexico. My mother is still there, I think."

"You think? I am sorry. You must think I'm nosy." She looked away.

"No ma'am. I just haven't been back for a long time." He did not mind anything she said to him. He had not had a conversation with a beautiful woman in a long time. "I brought some things for dinner, or breakfast."

She smiled at him appreciatively. "It's been a while since we've had any company. We don't need anything for dinner but we would be happy to share breakfast with you." She turned away to tend to the food she was cooking.

Jake and Jesse walked up with their arms full of small branches.

"Welcome to our camp." Jake smiled broadly.

"Thanks. I am lookin' forward to having a good meal. It's been a while." That was no lie he thought to himself.

"Anna is a good cook and she has made a fine stew for dinner." Jake smiled at his sister.

"Jonas brought us some bacon and eggs for breakfast."

"It sounds like we invited the right man to dinner. This almost reminds me of how it used to be when neighbors came by back home." Jake said enthusiastically.

"Can I play with your dog Mister?" Jesse asked.

"Sure. He's kind of shy but he won't bite." Jonas told the boy.

Just then, Anna interrupted. "Dinner is ready."

The four of them quietly ate as they appreciated the meal.

"I can't remember the last time I had food this good." Jonas commented.

"This is the best meal we've had for a while also. Good job sis." Jake added.

"Thank you both, that little store had some good vegetables to put in the stew so it wasn't all meat and beans for a change."

"Can I give the dog some food?" Jesse asked his mother.

"You should ask Jonas." She replied.

"Please. I used to have a dog." The boy said as he looked at the wolf sadly.

"Sure, he likes people food. His name is Cody. Don't give him very much or I'll have to fight him for it." Jonas smiled and called the wolf over and the boy offered him a plate with some stew on it. The wolf cautiously ate as the boy rubbed his head.

Jake looked at the scene and smiled. "We had to leave Jesse's dog behind when we set out for California. He misses him a lot."

"I understand. Cody is better company than most people I meet." Jonas sincerely added.

"I can relate to that." Jake laughed.

"I've got some dried venison in my saddlebags. Follow me Jesse and you can give Cody his dinner, this stew is too good to waste on him."

Jesse jumped up and followed Jonas.
After dinner was cleared up, Anna sent Jesse to bed in the wagon and the three of them sat by the fire and enjoyed the last of the hot coffee.

"I'll take the watch for first half of the night and then I'll wake you." Jonas told Jake.

"That's nice of you. I was getting kind of nervous about being here after we went in the saloon. I feel much safer now." Replied Jake then continued.

"I'll leave the place next to Jesse for when you come to bed Anna." Jake went to the back of the wagon to climb in.

"Why are you folks headin' to California?" Jonas asked Anna after Jake went to bed.

"Five years ago Jake and I lived in Kansas City with our parents. I met my husband, Eric, and after he asked me to marry him, we planned to move to Denver where his parents lived. My father was a schoolteacher and he always wanted to see the ocean so when they were getting ready to leave my mother and father decided to take the train out to California. They asked Jake if he wanted to go with them or stay with Eric and me until they got settled in and he chose to stay with us. When Eric and I moved to Denver, we started a clothing store with the help of his parents. I am good at designing and sewing clothing and Eric's father was a big merchant so Eric did the buying and Jake worked at the store. We became successful and my parents kept writing to us that Los Angeles was growing fast and that if we moved there. We could open an emporium out there and do even better than we had in Denver. Therefore, we decided to leave our store with Eric's parents running it and move to California to start a new one. The things my father wrote about California sounded amazing. He said it was warm and sunny all of the time and that the ocean was the most impressive thing he had ever seen in his life. Eric, Jake, Jesse and I left Denver a couple of months ago and decided to come by wagon." Jonas carefully listened as she continued,

"We brought some things we will need for our new store and some things my parents left behind. The rest of our stuff we are going to have sent by train once we get a place to put them. It seemed like a neat adventure. Now I wish we had taken the train but we can't turn back now." Anna sounded scared and depressed.

"I haven't been to California but I've heard it's a wonderful place. I do not think they have to worry much about Indians out there either. The place I am headed to is south of there. I know what you mean about wanting to do things differently. Sometimes I wish I had done that too, ma'am."

"Quit calling me ma'am, my name is Anna." She looked at him with fiery eyes.

"Yes ma...I mean Anna." She was so beautiful she was making him feel like a boy again. The way he felt with Victoria.

"Thank you. You make me feel like an old lady when you say ma'am." She smiled.

"You're no old lady and you're very pretty." He nervously told her.

"Thank you and you are a very polite man." She coyly looked at him.

"Not too many people would agree with you about

that." He was becoming tongue-tied. He had not flirted with a woman for a long time.

"I find that hard to believe." She smiled again.

"Believe it." He got up and put some more wood on the fire. He glanced at her and sat back down. They quietly watched the fire rise and fall and when it died down he put a little more wood on it and Anna got in the back of the wagon with her brother and son.

Jonas stood watch until the middle of the night when he woke up Jake to relieve him. Jonas laid on his bedroll next to the low burning fire and slept while Jake was on watch detail.

In the morning, Anna cooked the bacon and eggs along with sourdough pancakes for breakfast.

"This is the best breakfast I've had in years. I don't do much cooking for myself." Jonas said.

"It's just the food you brought us." She smiled and looked down. "And I'm grateful you did. We haven't had a proper breakfast since we left Denver."

"You're a good man to know!" Jake slapped him on the back.

"I liked the bacon best." Jesse added and took off with a piece to give to Cody.

"I'm glad you liked it. There is plenty more dried meat for Cody though. You ought to eat the bacon." Jonas replied.

"I'm going to go pack up the wagon. Stay and finish the coffee while I do," Jake got up and walked over to the wagon.

"How long have you been away from your home?" Anna inquired.

"It's been almost ten years."

"Why did you leave, if you don't mind me asking?"

"It sounds kind of silly now but I was in a gunfight over a girl with someone I thought was a friend and I lost. We all three grew up as friends on the same ranch. Rafael's mother was Victoria's father's cook, after her mother died; my mother became her father's wife a couple years after my father was killed in an accident. Victoria and I were thirteen when my mother married her father. Rafael was three years older than we were, and he was in love with Victoria but she had grown up with him and thought of him as a brother. Rafael was determined to have Victoria and had been practicing to be a gunfighter. One day when I was sixteen, he made me draw on him in a fight over Victoria. He drew faster and shot first, he left me for dead and took Victoria away from the ranch. I have been searching for them ever since. I became fast with a gun so I can beat him if I ever find them."

"That's a sad story. Do you know where they are?"

"I recently heard of a gunfighter in Mexico with the name of Rafael who has a beautiful woman with him. It may not be him but I need to find out. If it's not him I'm ready to quit searching."

"You have been looking for a long time." She seemed amazed.

"Yes. It seems kind of stupid now but I can't stop yet. Meeting a woman like you makes me think I should have quit a long time ago though." Jonas gave her a shy smile.

"That's sweet of you to say. That woman is lucky." She gave him what he perceived as a seductive smile.

"I don't know about that or if she even cares about me anymore. She probably thinks I'm dead." He said disappointedly and looked at the ground.

Jake and Jesse came walking up. "We have the wagon packed up and ready to go. Do you want to travel along with us to California?" Jake asked Jonas.

"Sure, your sister is too good of a cook for me to say no. Besides, two guns are better than one." Jonas was interested for more reasons than the food.

"That's a good point. I look forward to your company on the trail." Jake responded.

Jonas and the family headed on through the rest of Arizona and into California. The landscape went from brush and creeks to desert and then to lush grass and trees. Jonas took Jesse out on hunting trips with him and Cody as they traveled. By the time, they got close to Los Angeles they were back to the desert again. They enjoyed a lot of venison and rabbit roasted on the campfire at the end of the day. In the evenings Jake, Jonas and Anna visited around the fire while Jesse and Cody played games together. Usually it was chasing each other and fighting over a stick. It was a good time for all.

They encountered several more odd little towns much like the one they all met at but they seemed to draw less attention with the four of them traveling together than they had as a threesome or a solitary man with a gun. Anna and Jonas were becoming increasingly attracted to each other.

Late one afternoon Anna was getting dinner ready while Jake and Jonas were tending to the horses and mules. Anna wondered over to where the men were to tell them dinner was almost ready but stopped when she heard her name mentioned.

"Anna is getting pretty fond of you I hope you know."

"She is a great cook and pretty sweet to look at." Jonas responded softly. "I am getting hungry just thinking about her cooking."

"Is that all you're getting hungry for?" Jake teasingly said. Then he saw Anna standing by the wagon. "Hiya sis!"

Jonas looked up startled that she might have heard them talking about her. Jake led the mules to the tie line and left her and Jonas alone.

"I heard you say you were hungry. Dinner is almost ready." She gave him a small smile.

"I am." He gently put his arm over her shoulder and gently pulled her close. He softly put his lips against hers and kissed her. Her lips were soft, just as if he had imagined them to be. She kissed him back, they lingered with their lips for a moment, and then she blushingly looked down. "We should go eat," she said and walked back to the fire.

Jonas started to wonder if there was any point in pursuing Rafael and Victoria but he still felt driven to finish his search after having been on his quest for so long. Jesse and Cody had become inseparable buddies and Jonas felt that when he needed to leave Cody would be better off staying with his new friends because if Rafael was as good as his reputation Cody might be without anyone to care for him.

Despite the warnings about Indians, they very rarely saw any, when they did there were no confrontations. They only ventured into settlements and towns when they really needed supplies to accompany the meat.

The four of them finally arrived in Los Angeles and Jake and Anna's parents had been very welcoming when they finally arrived. After a few weeks Jonas became very fond of the entire family, he missed his and the good times he had with the family he had left behind in New Mexico. Sleeping on a real bed every night was pretty easy to get used to as well as not having to travel. He missed his mother and even though he occasionally sent a letter to her he hadn't received any back because he never stayed in one location long enough to get one back. He almost wrote one but he decided to wait and see if he made it back from Mexico. If he did, he swore that he would go back and visit her.

While staying with Anna and Jake's family Jonas started enquiring around about the town he heard Rafael was living in. He discovered that he would have been better off to head straight down to Mexico from his home in New Mexico. It sort of made sense when he thought about it. Rafael took Victoria and as far away as he could as fast as he could. When Jonas announced he was heading back towards New Mexico to go south, Jake volunteered to ride with him. Jonas tried to discourage him but Jake was bored with Los Angeles and was intrigued to go and visit the rugged country of Mexico. Jonas enjoyed Jake's company so he allowed his accompany him, they set out for what could be a month or more expeditions before they would return, if they returned. Anna begged them not to go but they did not listen to her.

"I know I have no right to ask you to stay so I won't." She looked at Jonas with tears in her eyes.

"Anna, don't cry. I love you. I know you do not understand why I need to finish this journey but I do. It is not that I still want Victoria back but that I want Rafael to pay for costing me all these years I spent searching for him. I know that makes no sense. It's a stupid man thing!" He was trying his best to keep her calm.

"I do understand but that doesn't mean I want you to go. I am glad Jake is going with you. I feel like you will be safer together. I'll be waiting for you to return and no matter what you decide to do I will accept it." She gave him a kiss.

"I will come back, even if it is to say goodbye. You deserve that much and more. I am pleased to have your brother's company but I vow that he will return no matter what happens to me. I want Cody to stay here with Jesse because I don't know what we'll be going into and he may get shot." He waited for confirmation from her.

"Of course, I'm not sure Jesse would let you take him anyway." She smiled.

"Thank you. Cody has been my buddy for a long time and he deserves a loving place to live." Jonas kissed her again and headed out to finish getting his horse ready. They were taking one mule with lots of supplies because they knew it was a long journey ahead and they did not know if there was going to be any places to get anything in the deserts of Mexico.

As they rode along in silence, Jonas thought back to

the beginning of his journey.

He was having trouble, picturing Victoria but he knew he would recognize Rafael, his memory being kept alive by hatred and thoughts of revenge.

Victoria was the daughter of Fernando, a wealthy Mexican rancher, who had owned the ranch next to his family and after Jonas's father died suddenly after an accident Victoria's father helped his mother take care of the ranch. She and her Jonas soon moved to Fernando's ranch to help his wife, who had become ill, care for their house and daughter. A couple of years later she became his wife after Victoria's mother died. Jonas and Victoria were thirteen years old when their parents got married to each other.

Rafael was the son of Fernando's cook and he grew up on the ranch alongside Victoria, he was three years older and he was in love with her but she thought of him as a brother. When Jonas and his mother moved to the ranch Victoria became very enamored of the cute young son. Rafael was not pleased with Victoria's relationship with Jonas. Rafael was already working as a cowboy on the ranch and was out on the range all day, which left Jonas and Victoria alone around the house, and corrals where Jonas helped with the horses her father raised. He had some beautiful horses and Jonas had proved himself a natural when it came to handling them. Rafael was also good with the horses but he did not get to hang out on the ranch all day like Jonas did. Rafael was treated more like a hired hand and Jonas more like a son, which also did not set too well with Rafael since he was there first.

Jonas thought Victoria was the most beautiful girl he had ever seen, not that he had been around many girls. Competing with Jonas for Victoria's attention made Rafael come to hate Jonas and Rafael practiced to become fast with a gun hoping someday he would have a chance to challenge him to a gun fight and win Victoria for his own. Jonas was aware that Rafael hated him, although when he first moved to the ranch they had been friends but that was before Victoria and he became so close.

Their rivalry came to a head when Rafael was twenty and caught Victoria and Jonas kissing in the stable. That was when he decided to goad Jonas into a gunfight. Jonas accepted and unbeknownst to their mothers they picked a time to meet out behind the barn when they both knew everyone would be preoccupied. Neither one of them told Victoria about the fight but she had been suspicious when she saw them whispering. She watched them walk out to the horse corrals behind the barn, followed them, and watched as they faced each other and turned and walked away from each other. She figured out what they were doing and ran out into the corral.

"What are you doing?" She yelled at them as they went their twenty paces from each other.

"Get out of here." Jonas said.

"Why? So you can shoot each other?" She was frantic.

"Don't worry I will win." Rafael said.

"I don't want anyone to win." She said.

"It's too late for that. I met you first." Rafael replied.

"What difference does that make?" She looked from one to the other.

"I loved you first. He can't have you." Rafael told her.

"Who said either one of you could have me?" She told him.

"You should get out of here. This is between Rafael and me." Jonas told her.

"No it's not. It is between all of us. I don't want you to fight for me." She was pleading for them to stop.

Jonas looked at her. "I am fighting because he is disrespectful, not because of you."

As the two young men stood and prepared to draw their guns Victoria could see, she could not stop the fight and ran off to get the help of her father. As soon as she ran around the barn, she heard a gun go off and ran back. She saw Jonas lying on the ground and Rafael walking up to him.

"I'm sorry. He drew on me as soon as you ran off." Rafael said to her.

Victoria turned and ran to get her father, and by the time, she got around the barn her father along with Jonas and Rafael's mothers were already headed to the corral where the gunshots came from.

Rafael was standing over Jonas and he looked at everyone running towards him. "He pushed me into drawing on him, I didn't want to."

"Get out of here. I can't believe I took you into my home." Victoria's father said to him.

Rafael looked around at everyone who was staring at him. "Believe me Victoria; I didn't want to fight him."

Jonas was lying on the ground helplessly watching Rafael lie to Victoria, he had drawn and shot Jonas as soon as Victoria had run around the corner of the barn and Jonas had turned his head to watch her. She just stood there frozen. Rafael walked over to her and hugged her. He pulled her towards him. She started crying and held on to him. He took advantage of her weakness and guided her towards two horses that were saddled and tied in front of the house.

"Come with me querida and I will take care of you." Rafael put her on the horse and rode off with her before anyone could get to them as they were all gathered around the fallen Jonas.

The gunshot had knocked the air out of Jonas's lungs and he could not say a thing as he watched Rafael spirit Victoria away. By the time he could speak, it was too late. They carried Jonas to the house and someone went to bring the doctor back. The bullet had only penetrated his chest a few deep inches missing any vital organs it was easily removed and sewn up. After several weeks of mending, he was furious about what happened and that the family had allowed Rafael to leave with Victoria.

No one had any idea where Rafael had taken Victoria. Since Rafael had fancied himself a great gunfighter Jonas hoped that one day, he would hear of him shooting someone else and find him. Jonas had worked his way through New Mexico and Arizona and recently someone told him they saw a man called Rafael in a gunfight in Sedona and that he had come from a little town just the other side of the Mexican border. This was just before he met Jake, Anna and Jesse.

Jonas and Jake rode back through Arizona towards New Mexico and then down the Mexican desert. It took them several weeks before they got past the desert and encountered the jungle where they expected to find the town with Rafael. They were pleasantly surprised to find the people in the tiny villages they rode into along the way were very friendly and shared many meals with them. They usually would not even take any money. They ate some interesting new foods they had never had before, hot, spicy and very flavorful accompanied by flavorful liquor called Tequila.

Finally, Jonas was sure they were riding into the place they were looking for. It was getting dark and they noticed an unusual pattern of light up ahead. As they rode closer, they could see a cross up ahead. They had finally discovered the place called La Cruz, called that because there were candles burning in the shape of a cross. It was the sign they were looking for. They made their camp for the evening outside the shrine of candles.

"This is an amazing place!" Jake said.

"It certainly is its beautiful here now that we are out of the desert. Let us eat the food we bought from that little village for dinner and celebrate with some Tequila. If I find Rafael tomorrow this may be my last meal." Jonas flashed a smile at Jake who did not smile back.

"Don't talk like that. My sister will be very mad at me if I come home alone!"

"It wouldn't surprise me if we don't find Rafael and Victoria and turn around and head home tomorrow."

"As far as I'm concerned we could do that as soon as we get up tomorrow."

"You are welcome to head back in the morning but I've come too far to do that."

"I know."

Jonas and Jake saw some shadowy figures walking around the shrine of the cross as they lay near it and tried to get some sleep. The next morning they had some jerky and coffee and rode towards the pristine beach, which was on the other side of the bluff the cross was on. The sand stretched out for miles with no visible human life anywhere on it. Jonas and Jake made their way down the shoreline until they got near an old hotel they could see from the beach. It looked like the one they had been told to go to.

They started towards it on the path through the jungle, which encroached upon the sand with its large tropical trees and dense foliage. As the trail got closer to the large foreboding building there were several small trails that broke off, none headed directly for the hotel. One led them to a river that flowed towards the ocean with an inlet with a crocodile sunning itself on a log along with Iguanas, turtles and snowy egrets. Jonas and Jake were amazed by what they were seeing.

"I wish Anna could be with us. This is the most beautiful place I have ever seen!" Jake said in awe as he looked around.

"Yes it is amazing! I'm sure she would enjoy seeing this, maybe next time," Jonas caught Jake's eyes and smiled.

"Right, next time."

They turned around, went back, and took the other fork in the trail and as they walked their horses through the mangroves and other jungle plants, they suddenly came across large piles of carcasses of strange large creatures alongside the trail. The horses were spooked at these mounds of rotting flesh.

"What the hell are these things?" Jake was fighting to keep his horse walking forward.

"I've never seen anything like these before! Looks like something out of a bad dream." Jonas got his horse to walk up to the piled up creatures.

The giant bodies were several feet wide and they were stacked about ten deep in several locations off to the side of the path they had been walking their horses through it all. The horses were nervously reacting to the smell of death. They looked like fish but were large winged looking creatures with tails that resembled a scorpion.

"They look like deformed giant fish!" Jonas said.

"Look part of their backs have been carved out."

"Why would someone do that I wonder?"

"I don't know why anyone would want any part of a creature like this." Replied Rafael.

"This is strange. Maybe we should leave."

"I still need to find out if Rafael and Victoria are here. You are still welcome to go back." Jonas was determined to keep on going.

"I know. Just the same I would like to get out of here."

"Let's get to the hotel." Jonas said and spurred his horse on.

They kept on the trail and suddenly there was clearing in the jungle that contained the large old hotel. From the beach, it had looked marvelous. It was huge, white and resembled a giant Mexican mansion. Up close, it looked like the ruins they had been told it was. It had obviously been magnificent once upon a time.

They stopped their horses in front of the building and a young boy came running out. "Are you here to spend the night?" The boy asked them.

"No. We are looking for someone who lives here."

Jonas answered.

"Who?" The boy looked at them curiously.

"I'm looking for a man named Rafael and a woman named Victoria." Jonas told the boy.

"They are here. You need to get off the beach. It is time for the jejenes to come." The boy looked distressed.

"Time for what to come?" Jake asked.

"The meat eating sand flies. They don't like smoke so we light fires and stay inside until they leave the beach."

"Lead us to where we need to be then. We will follow." The boy led them behind the hotel into a courtyard. There were several boys lighting piles of brush in semi-circle around the building. The boy motioned for them to follow, he walked through the smoky circle to a large enclosure covered with large leaves from the trees, and there was an entryway the boy disappeared through.

Jonas and Jake dismounted, quickly surrounded by a cloud of biting insects. The horses started to jump all around and the men quickly led them between the piles of smoky brush following the boy. Once past the smoky brush and through the hanging leaves the insects were no longer around and the horses calmed. The boy motioned them to keep moving forward and he led them into another structure inside the large complex. There were stalls with other horses inside and the boy led them to an open stall.

"Put the horses in there, they will be safe. Follow me." Jonas and Jake did as they were told. After the horses were safely inside the boy led them to the center of the hotel. As they entered the building, they were amazed at how large the enclosed courtyard was. The rock walls were twenty feet tall with small covered openings to let in the light.

"Hello my old friend. I was wondering when you would show up." A deep voice said and Jonas looked around to see a dark figure in the entryway. The man stepped into the light. He was dressed in black and wearing pearl handled revolvers on both hips. Rafael looked much older but Jonas immediately recognized him.

"I've been looking for you for a long time." Jonas stared intensely at Rafael.

Jake stood there quietly watching. He had heard the story and was not sure what was going to occur.

"I've been here ever since we left New Mexico. You aren't really looking for me are you?" Rafael calmly said.

"Yes I am. You shot me, left me for dead and took Victoria. I owe you for not finishing the job."

"Does that mean you wanted to die? I was not trying to kill you, just to make Victoria think you were dead so she would leave with me. I needed to get her away from you so she could see that she really loved me." Rafael's lips curled to form a small smile.

"Do you really expect me to believe that? I didn't want to die but if you had killed me I wouldn't have had to waste the last ten years looking for you!" Jonas started to walk towards Rafael. Jake looked at him for instructions as to what to do. Jonas motioned for him to stay out of it.

"Believe what you want. I knew Victoria first and she was mine. I did not tell you to come looking for us. The revenge you seek is on you. We've been very happy here." Rafael kept his eyes on Jonas and started walking a large circle around him while keeping his eyes on Jake.

"Shouldn't she have had a say in what happened?" Jonas asked as he slightly turned his body to keep Rafael in his direct line of site.

"She did, I asked if she wanted to leave with me." He replied.

"You mean after she thought I was dead? Some choice!" Jonas took a couple of steps forward. Jake nervously backed up.

"It doesn't matter now; she made her choice a long time ago. I do not want to fight you again. I won and it is over as far as I am concerned. Would you like to see Victoria or did you just come here to shoot me?" Rafael looked at him, turned, and walked over to the doorway he had come through. He looked at Jake. "Well, what would you like to do?"

"I'll stay with the horses."

"Victoria is here?" Jonas followed Rafael towards the exit from the courtyard.

"Of course she's here. She has always been here with me. I know she would like to see you. She was quite fond of you." Rafael continued walking.

Jonas followed Rafael as he walked out of the courtyard and into a hallway that led to some rooms in the large stone building.

"This place was built by the Spanish after they built their fort on the cliffs. They wanted a place they could easily access from their ships. No one was living here when Victoria and I arrived so with the help of some of the local fisherman, who also needed places to live, we rebuilt it to keep the biting bugs away and out of the rooms. Many people live here now, most of the men fish, which is also what I do."

"You are a fisherman? I thought you were going to be a wild horse tamer?"

"I only did that because you were so good at it. I wanted Victoria to look at me the way she looked at you." Rafael led the way to a room and opened the door.

Jonas cautiously followed him inside. It was very large and looked out over the beach and jungle he had ridden through to get there. "You have a nice view."

"Yes I do. I saw you and your friend ride in from the beach. It is a beautiful place, yes?"

"Yes it is. I thought you were bringing me to Victoria."

"I am she is in one of the other rooms. I will go get her." Rafael walked over to one of the many doors in the large room. He opened the door and stood there as two children came running through the door, a boy dressed in all white clothing about seven and a girl with a bright yellow dress at about five. Rafael disappeared through the door and Victoria walked out into the room.

"Jonas, how wonderful to see you." She was still a beautiful woman and she looked very happy.

Jonas was speechless. He had been on this journey of revenge so long he never stopped to really think about what the new reality might be. "You look beautiful. I wasn't sure I would ever see you again."

"I knew I would see you. Rafael confessed that he made you fight him after we got here. At first, I was mad but he told me he did it because he had always been in love with me and he was afraid you were the one I loved and that he would lose me. Then he told me he knew he was sure he only wounded you and that you would be all right, although he told me you were dead when he first convinced me to leave with him. He told me you shot first and missed but later confessed it was the other way around. He had said he had removed some of the gunpowder from the casing to weaken the load; he really did not want you to die. I wrote my father a letter and asked him what happened to you after we arrived here. He wrote me back, said that you were fine, and that you took off looking for Rafael and I.

I knew you would find us here someday. Especially since my father and your mother write us letters. I expected them to tell you where we were."

"The joke is on me. I write letters to my mother but I never stay in one place long enough for her to write me back. I am glad you are doing well. Your children are beautiful." Jonas was beginning to feel very stupid.

The boy's name is Samuel our son he is six years old now and my daughter there is two years old, her name is Carmella.

"Are you going to fight Rafael?" She asked him with a worried look.

"That's what I came here to do. The truth is that it does not seem to matter anymore. I wanted revenge for being shot and for him taking you. But why fight for a woman who no longer wants me."

"I was young. I did think I loved you but I came to realize I had always loved Rafael. I do not want to lose either one of you. Is there anything I can say to stop you from fighting?"

"No. You do not need to say anything. It is over. I've wasted too many years chasing after you two and it's time to quit." Jonas actually had a feeling of contentment wash over him. He had a good friend waiting to accompany him back to California where a beautiful woman and a young boy who needed a father were waiting for both of them.

"Why don't we bring your friend up here so we can have dinner?" Rafael said from the doorway where he was watching the reunion.

Rafael called out for his servant, "Lucio!"

"Si, señor Rafael what is it I can do for you?"

Lucio was a smallish man dressed in the usual white shirt, short pants with rope belt and sandals. Atop his head sat a straw sombrero with a shiny silver band around it.

"I want you to go and bring the other visitor inside we have invited them to stay for dinner?" Rafael said.

"Si, Si, señor right away." Lucio limped away through the door with a guitar upon his back.

"We can't stay very long but I suppose we can stay for dinner, and leave in the morning. Since you are now a fisherman what are all those strange dead creatures that we passed on the way here, the ones that look like huge scorpions?" Jonas asked.

"They are called Rayos and only a small portion of them is good to eat. The fishermen take out that part and stack the rest of them in a pile. Then they take them and use them for bait to catch better things, there are many creatures that are good to eat on the bottom of the ocean. We never had this many kinds of fish to eat in New Mexico. We live on the things we get out of the ocean here. It's an amazing place." Rafael was quite animated.

"Yeah I've already heard that." Jonas was being honest as Anna and Jake's father had been very excited about what that the ocean had to offer when they had first met. Things seemed to be coming full circle. It was time for him to go back and pay a visit to see his mother, after he and Jake returned to California to Anna and Jesse.

Lucio stopped them, may I play you one song for you and your travels before you leave?"

Jonas looked at Jake, and Jake nodded his approval.
Lucio pulled his guitar around and began to play for them.
♪Two young men loved one woman
Together where they live
One day there was a dual
A man's life he'd give,
As two lovely ones parted
One remained to live
Vowing his hatred revenged
Now they find each other
His hate it be unhinged
Anna she shall be the one
Jonas a father to her Son…♪

"Thank you Lucio that was a beautiful and fitting song." Said Jonas.
They mounted their horses and headed back North.

Jake and Jonas looked back at the little man and the family waving a long goodbye.
Jake had noticed the estranged look on Jonas' face.
"What's up with that look?" he asked.
"How did that little fellow who sung that song know Anna's name?"
"That is strange, maybe just a lucky guess?"

CHAPTER 23

The Sound of Redemption

The following month Bode was taking a prisoner up to El Paso for trial there. About five miles out of town, Bode came upon a lone horseman standing steadfast in the middle of the road. As he and his prisoner slowly rode up on him, Bode stiffened in his saddle as he recognized the man immediately.

It was Eric Desmond.
As Bode rode closer, he noticed something else. Eric had a rifle trained on him.

"That's far enough, Johnson!" hollers Desmond.

"Eric, don't do anything stupid." said Bode as he stops his horse about a hundred feet away from the armed Desmond.

"Shut up, Johnson" he said with a bit of confidence. "I have been waiting for the opportunity to settle our score, and today's the day Marshal. The sarcastic tone used on the word 'marshal' gave Bode all he needed to know about how much respect Eric Desmond had for the law.

"That's right, it's Marshal now," said Bode sitting up straighter in the saddle. "This star means you better…" Johnson is cut off by the angry words of Desmond.

"That tin badge don't mean squat to me, Johnson. We are not in town and you are not the law out here, I am. You killed my brothers and I am fixing to make it right. Get off your horse now."

"I'm afraid I can't do that, Eric!" said Bode, now leaning casually on his saddle horn with both forearms. "You see I got me a prisoner here who's got to face trial up in El Paso for murder."

Eric looks beyond Johnson to the burly man on the horse. The man has a hardened look about him and just sits there chewing on an unlit thick hand rolled cigar, a slight grin on his face.

"That true?" he asks the prisoner. "You kill someone?"

The man takes his sweet time in responding to Eric.

"That's what they say," he said in a slow drawl.

"What they say . . . but what do you say?" asked Desmond resting the rifle across his left forearm still sighted on Johnson.

The prisoner gives a short chuckle.

"Well mister, I say. . . I ain't never killed nothing or nobody that did not have it coming to 'em."

Desmond smiles.

"I agree."

CRACK!

The prisoner's head snaps back violently the back of his skull blowing outward with brain and bone chunks. He then slumps to the left and slides off the horse hitting the ground with a sickening wet thud.

Johnson flinches at the rifle's report and the blood splattering his face. He quickly regains his composure, shaking his head but keeping a steady stare on Desmond. He knew he could not show Desmond any fear.

"Now why'd you go and do a fool thing like that, Eric?"

"He was guilty. I just saved the town of El Paso the cost of a trial, that's all."

"You know it doesn't have to go down this way," admonitions Johnson.

"Oh this ain't gonna go the way it did last time, lawman. This time you are going to be the one receiving a funeral. First you get it and then that no good Randy Reeder."

Bode knew the longer he could keep him engaged in banter the better off his chance's were for a favorable outcome.

"C'mon Eric, killing a Marshal? That will bring all kinds of law down on you. To kill a lawman in these parts and you might as well put the noose around your neck yourself, you should know that."

Eric looks around to see no one is near he returns his stare back to Johnson with a grin.

"The only witness to this here party is lying there taking a 'Dirt Nap.'

"No Johnson, you are the only one to die but it will be legal-like. Now get off your horse."

Bode dismounts, wary to keep a watchful eye on his assailant once down he takes a few steps away from his horse then stops.

"You sure this is what you want to do, Eric?"

"Shut up! I swear, Johnson. . . I don't see what Mica sees in you."

This statement caught Bode like a mule kick to the head.

"Yeah, didn't think I knew about you and her, did you?" he said with an arrogant smile. "Maybe after I'm done I'll just ride back to town and let her know what she's been missing.

"You know I almost asked her to marry me, did she tell

you that? No, I do not suppose she did. Well turns out she fancies herself some top shelf lady or something, too good for the likes of ole' Eric Desmond. Wonder how she would feel when I tell her that her man begged for his life like a dog. Heh, heh."

Bode's faced drained of all emotion. He now stared at Desmond with dark tenacity.

"You see Johnson; I make it a habit to know about the men who kill my kin. You? You are a hard case, a real piece of work you are a wanted man in seven territories. Now you are a Marshal, imagine that."

Bode let his eyes wander to the gun trained on him.

"But you've played out your stake Mister Bode Johnson, and now you're done. It is all over. You see I know about your little secret. I know your real name!"

Johnson's eyes rose slowly to again meet Desmond' as Eric continued his rant. Bode's index finger was tapping against the handle of his Colt revolver now.

"I know you're not what you claim to be. I know who you are…

CRACK!

Bode Johnson now watches stoically as Eric Desmond staggers backwards, raising his hand to his chest He looks at Bode, his jaw ajar and his eyes wide with disbelief. Slowly he drops to his knees his right index finger squeezing the trigger of his rifle, firing off a round harmlessly into the dirt. Bode continued watching as Desmond's eyes roll upwards. Eric convulses then falls face first into the road. A cloud of dust springs up around him as he breathes his last.

Johnson stands there silently, his gun at his hip pointed towards Desmond, bluish smoke drifting from its barrel.

As much as he had hoped differently, he knew this was how it was going to end. Desmond's own petulance had cost the life a man whose personal safe travel was entrusted to Johnson by the law. Now Eric Desmond is dead as well, Bode Johnson has two corpses to deal with.

He lifted and tied both bodies to their respective horses and headed back to town. This was something entirely different for Bode Johnson. He had always been on the other side of the star. He has always been the outlaw on the run, always looking over his shoulder for a man with a badge or someone looking to claim the bounty on his head. Now he was the one standing behind the badge. He was the one chasing the outlaws. He was the one with the law on his side.

It was a new and unsettling feeling yet one that filled his heart with pride and purpose. Finally, he would found a way to atone for all that he had done wrong in his life. This irony being on the side of good after so long on the side of bad was not lost on Bode Johnson in the least. However, he liked it and he embraced it despite it's sometimes, repugnant side. He knew that in the end he did only what he had to do and in the months to come, peace would finally settle on the troubled soul of Bode Johnson.

While he was enjoying his new lease on life, he could not help but feel like a piece was missing. Mica O'Shea was the only woman he had ever spent any meaningful amount of time. All the women in his previous life were nothing more than fleeting fancies, bordello flies flitting about his life, only to be eventually swatted away.

Not Mica, she had become the sun and moon in Bode Johnson's world. She was the reason he woke in the morning.

She was his last thought before falling asleep at night she was his hope, his wish, his very breath that kept his heart beating.

CHAPTER 24

The midday sun glinted off the five-pointed Marshal's star pinned to Bode Johnson's dusty weathered black leather vest as he stepped from his office onto the creaky wooden boardwalk. Although it has been many months since he took to the badge, still the job of a law officer had not been what he thought he would be doing upon coming to the town. Life and circumstance sure do make for funny bedfellows. He chuckled under his breath as he stepped down into the dusty street.

The old church bell rang out loudly beckoning all with the One o'clock hour.

In the southern sky, darkening clouds begin drifting in as if threatening to swallow up the sun. Within a half hour the clouds had increased and the sky began giving the appearance of a gray dusk on the town. It was as if something bad were making its way into town.

It had been almost a month since they buried a third of the town's residents after the attack by Maxwell, and life had nearly returned to its mundane normalcy but today the winds of change seem to blow into town with something almost tangibly malicious on their currents.

Bode Johnson sat in the Steele Point Diner eating his lunch. He has kept a watchful eye on the gathering clouds outside. He casually glanced around the dining room.

STEELE CREEK

There were just five people in the joint on what would normally be a very busy day. Mica O'Shea working the kitchen, Bill Fortin the owner, Randy Reeder, the cattle rancher, Grady Gaston, another rancher and Joey Cross, sitting in the back corner playing solitaire. Bode chuckles to himself and returns his attention his meal.

By one-forty-five, he had finished most of his meal and was just picking over the last bits of steak and potatoes. He glanced back out the large glass window. His brow creased a bit with confusion. The wind was whipping wildly now. The sky was fully overcast with ominous gray clouds. The dust and sand flying about so thick it nearly blotted out the afternoon sun.

CHAPTER 25

Dust Devil

Bode looked down the street and could barely see a block because of the sandstorm. He had seen terrible dust storms in his travels through, New Mexico and Arizona but this one seemed different. It did not just feel different. It was different. The streets were empty now as the town's folk hurried to shelter. Old Man Whalen stumbled in, coughing and hacking, his lungs trying to expunge the dust.

"Gotdamn!" he spit. "It's like ole' Scratch himself stirring up the damned out there! Cannot see a foot in front of your face, by Jesus! Gimme a beer for Christ sakes!"

Old Man Whalen was the oldest living Steele Creek resident at seventy-one. He had been around so long that there is no one left that does not remember him not always living in Steele Creek. He was an affable old fellow with a keen eye and sharper wit. Spending most of his time helping at the Dry Goods store or delivering mail about the town.

Bode stared at Whalen as he shook off the dust from his clothes and wiped the sand from his eyes, the old man takes his regular seat at the bar. Most people said to anyone else who had tried to sit there that they only had one minute to move or face the wrath of Ole' Whalen.

Although they knew Whalen posed no threat, there was uneasiness in Bode and the others that they could not shake as he turned his gaze back out the window.

"It's awfully dark out there. Is it a Dust Devil, you think?" Bill asked Whalen.

"Damned if I know," he said slapping his hat against his leg to knock away the dust. "It ain't like it's swirling around twister-like. It is more like it is coming right down the street, straight and hot. He spit out the sand from his mouth into the brass spittoon on the floor at his feet, shit who knows what it is for sure?"

Bode smiled slightly at the notion. Even so, he could not help but feel somehow connected to the storm as if it somehow followed him or searching for him. He laughed under his breath and shook the thought from his mind, shoveling the last spoonful of beans into his mouth.

"What in tarnation?" said Randy Reeder as he stared out the window, "What in the hell is that idiot think he's doing?"

Bode dropped his napkin onto his plate. He took a healthy swig of his coffee and peered out into the gathering darkness. A movement in the distance caught his eye. He stared intently trying to discern just what it was as a shape made its way slowly down the street. When it got about a block and a half away, he could make out a figure on horseback coming in from the west and heading straight up the avenue amidst the pummeling sandstorm. Bode squinted hard trying to make out any details of the figure but could not.

That damned fool's going to suffocate out there he thought to himself. The figure stood as if a shadow with no perceptible features or details apparent it was as if the figure itself was made up of shadows instead of a real body. The horse was of the same indiscernible detail, no recognizable features visible to the human eye. The outlines of the entities seemed to be even more obscured through the pelting sandstorm. Bode felt the uneasiness return to the pit of his stomach.

"Now who do you suppose that is?" Reeder queried.

"Probably some idiot too stupid to know enough to get out of that storm." offered Cross from the back of the room.

"He's a horn-cracked fool if he's out in that ruckus," spits old man Whalen.

The horse and shadowy figure continued there procession down Main Street.

"Undoubtedly a saddle bum looking for a hand out, if you ask me" Bode said in a matter-of-fact tone as he watched the figure pass in front of the window. "He certainly not a bright fella if he's taken to Sunday-riding in the middle of sandstorms."

Abruptly the stranger stopped his horse in its tracks, almost as if he had overheard the words spoken about him by Bode. Through the large picture window, Bode curiously eyeballed the figure that was now right outside the front doors. He presses the newspaper flat on the table, trying to appear disinterested by the figure's eerie presence.

Mica O'Shea appears from the kitchen bring a plate of food for Whalen who is now seated at the bar. She slides the dish in front of him while noticing that everyone's attention is centered on the front window.

"What's everyone looking at?" she said with her usual effervescent smile.

"Some fella just marching his horse down Main Street in the middle of a dust devil like it was some foolish carnival parade." said Grady with a crooked toothed grin.

'A Dust Devil' Bode thought. The term seemed to bother him for some reason.

"What's he doing now?" Mica said curiously, as she walked over and stood beside Bode who was still seated at his table by the window.

"He just stopped right there in the middle of the street" Randy said staring out the window on the other side of the front doors. "What in the hell?"

"Really he's just sitting out there in the middle of a sandstorm?" Mica said with concern in her voice.

Bode could not resist the urge to get a better look this figure. He stood up and peered through the window at the figure. He was joined by Bill Fortin, both now gawking at the stranger through the window.

"Land sakes, someone's better get that fella in outta that storm," Mica said in obvious contempt for the rest of the group watching. She drew up her apron to cover her mouth and nose and opened the door.

"Mica! You do not know who that is! He could be trouble!" cautioned Bill Fortin.
Mica looked back at the gathered group peering out the windows with a look of disappointment.

"Mica!" yelled Bode his voice in a commanding tone. He suddenly felt an overwhelming sense of dread.

"He's probably just some poor soul who's lost his way in that frightful storm. He may even be hurt for all we know," she said as she disappeared through the door. Bode now took a stance of concern as he intently watched Mica walk to the edge of the boardwalk and then out into the street towards the mysterious figure.

"Can't make him out too well from here," Reeder said as he made his way to the front doors.

Against the pelting sandstorm, Mica struggled to look up at the mounted figure facing the storm's stinging rage. She paused, as If listening to the stranger. The figure never even seemed to move while Mica talked. He just sat there, still as death itself.

Mica seemed to shake her head and then quickly turned back running towards the saloon.

"Well let's see what he had to say," he said as he opened the door for Mica. She came rushing through the door, coughing and shaking the sand out of her light brown hair.

"Well Mica . . . what'd he say?" asked Grady waiting impatiently.

Bode returned his gaze back out the window into the darkness of the storm, still trying to make out any distinguishable characteristics. He tried not to let his imagination run wild with thoughts of some former enemy coming here to track him down and kill him for past wrongs.

Whoa, he thought snapping his stare from the dark figure to Mica. Nobody knows who I am. Nobody even saw me head outta San Verde that night. I am sure of it.

The group gathered around Mica, anxious and more than a bit nervous.

"Well? What'd he say?" asked Whalen.

"What does he want? Why's he here?" Interjected Cross.

"Mica? Mica, you okay woman?" Bill asked.
Mica kept her head down, trying to catch her breath.

"Well Mica?" asked Bode. He stared intently at her as she raised her head slowly. She lifted her eyes directly to Bode's stare. She had a pained expression on her face as she answered.

"I asked him what he wanted, he answered, just a name," she stammered nervously.

"A name what name? Who's name?" Johnson demanded.

Mica swallowed hard, her eyes watering up now.

"Your name Bode" She said with worry in her voice.

Bode felt as if he had been kicked in the gut by a mule. He had always dreaded this day since taking up roots here. He had come to fear that day when someone from his past would finally catch up to him. This man out there must be a hard and determined person to be able to withstand these conditions. Bode had tried hard over the last few months to live the life he would dreamed of and leave his past out in the unforgiving sands of the Texas deserts.

"Bode? Bode!" Mica yells.
Her shout snaps Johnson back to reality. He looks at Mica with a stern stare.

"You sure he said my name?" Johnson inquired intently, searching her eyes for any signs of uncertainty. She nodded, wiping the tears from her eyes.

"Did you get a good look at him . . . his face anything?" he asked already knowing the answer.
"I couldn't see his face, just..." Mica brought a trembling hand to her mouth.
Bode stared at her with dear impatience.
"Just what?" he demanded.

"Just his . . . eyes. His awful eyes!"
"His eyes?" asked Bode tilting his head in confusion.

"It was like he could stare a hole, right through me. There is something not right about him! There's something very wrong, very . . . wrong." She cried.

Bode Johnson looked back out the saloon's large window. He squinted as his gaze fixed on the stranger in the driving dust storm. Through the darkened squall, he could faintly see the figure's head. The stranger slowly turned his head as if looking directly at Johnson.
Bode drew in a sudden breath as his blood ran cold.

Suddenly his heart quickened, beating and he felt

weak behind the knees.

"Who is he, Bode?" asks Mica, a look of horrified worry on her face.

Johnson gradually returned to his table and slowly dumped himself into his chair. His face was gaunt and pale.

"You all right Bode?" said Randy Reeder. "You look like you've see a ghost!"

Bode sat silent. He stared down at the table as Mica's voice broke his concentration.

"Bode!" shouted Mica abruptly bringing Bode's attention back to the room.

"Wha...?" Bode said in a groggily manner.

"Who is he?" demands Mica.

"I-I don't know?" he replies nervously.

"Bull Hockey!" thunders Whalen in an angry tone. "This here fella rides through a gotdamn sandstorm, stops outside the very building you're in, said he's looking for you and you say you don't know the man? I ain't buying it, Johnson!"

"Stop it!" Mica shouts at Whalen. Whalen retreats to his meal shaking his head as he does so.

"Aw c'mon, Mica," Bill Fortin said turning to Mica. "You've gotta admit it sure seems mighty funny that this fella comes all the way out here hunting Bode and Bode claims he doesn't know him? Something's fishy right there and everyone here knows it."

All eyes now fall on Johnson. He rubs his stubble chin in contemplation, ignorant of the group now slowly gathering around him.

"Maybe he's an old friend?" adds Joey with a nervous smile. "Maybe he's an old family member come looking up his kin, eh?"

The group is puzzled over the thought. Johnson

himself breaks up the buzzing conversations.

"He ain't a friend or kin to me," Bode said with conviction. All eyes return to Bode as he stands up from his chair.

"Hey look, you're all getting uppity over nothing," said Joey Cross now getting up from his table. "I'm gonna go see what this fella's about. You are all making a fuss about nothing. You'll see."

"Joey, don't...!" shouts Mica. "Bode don't let him." Bode watches warily as Cross, looks him straight in the eye and then disappears through the doors and into the storm. Through the window, Joey can be seen approaching the man. The seconds seem like hours as they all watch Joey trying to converse with the mysterious figure.

'Who could it be? What does he want with me?' Bode ponders in his mind. His thoughts are interrupted as Joey stumbles through the door back into the saloon.

"Blah!" he said spitting out the dust from his mouth. "Well that wasn't any fun."

"Well? Who is he? Did you see his face? What'd he say?" asked Reeder.

"I couldn't see his face; he's got it covered with a black kerchief except for his eyes. All I could see was the whites of his eyes. Just shiny bright white eyes, spooky as all hell." Joey said shaking his head slightly disbelief.

Bode remained standing, staring out the window at the darkened figure sitting calmly upon his horse in the middle of the raging sands.

"Did he say anything?" asked Whalen.

"Hey Bode . . . you ever been to a town called San Verde?" asks Joey.

The name sends an electric jolt down Johnson's spine. He reacts with the quickness honed from his former profession.

"What did he say?" Johnson said in a calm but demanding fashion.

"Just 'San Verde' nothing else!" exclaims Cross.

CHAPTER 26

Remembering San Verde

The name hits Johnson like a lightning bolt streaking through his mind. Sudden flashes of memories explode in his mind with images of a long forgotten night.

They come as quick memory image flashes (≈), short quick and revealingly!

≈ A young woman in his arms they are in bed. Her lips are warm. Her embrace is inebriating.

≈ The bedroom door is kicked open. A silhouetted man stands in the doorway, the light of the hallway behind him. There is a glint of bright silver in his right hand as he raises it from his hip.

≈ The woman screams. He rolls out of the bed to the floor.

≈ A gunshot. He scrambles and finds his own gun and draws it.

≈ Another gunshot. The man falls to his knees, then face first to the floor.

≈ Bode stands over the dead man. He turns to the woman still in the bed.

≈ She is staring in horror at Bode. Bode's eyes lower from hers.

≈ There is blood on her chest. Bode screams.

"NO!" Bode screams, his lungs seemingly ready to burst.

"You don't look so good!" asks Joey with a puzzled look on his face, "you screamed out NO!"
Bode shanking his head hard as if trying to wake from a sleep.
"What, what Joey, did you speak?" he asks.

Joey was concerned but decided not to press Bode.
"I said its fine if you don't know anything about San Verde?" he asked again.
"I am sorry, Joey. I did not mean to snap at you! " Bode stammers.

"Look, Bode, if you say you don't know this fella or this place he named, fine. I believe you. Nevertheless, for whatever reason this guy said he knows you. You need to straighten this out," said Bill Fortin. "I don't need the likes of him scaring off my customers, you understand?"
Bode draws in a deep breath.

"You know, I think I better get back to the stables. This storm's probably spooking the horses something fierce," Grady Gaston said as he grabs his Stetson from its wall hook, pulling his collar up tight around his neck. "I'll stop by the jail and send Denis up here just in case you need a hand with this fella, Bode."

Grady's eyes meet Bode's and the Marshal nods slightly. Grady smiles, makes his way to the front door and disappears through it
CRACK!
CRACK!

Two gun reports break the eerie silence of the saloon as they all watch the door. Seconds later Grady stumbles through the door, falling face first to the floor with a resounding wet thump.
"What the hell?" hollers Whalen from the bar, "Grady,

Grady you okay, he shot you?"

Mica rushes to his side and rolls Grady over onto his back.

"Are you hurt? We heard shots!" said Randy Reeder rushing to Grady's side.
Grady was certain the bullets entered his stomach and passed through him, as he reaches for his stomach to stem the flow of blood and hold his guts in.
He finds nothing, no blood, no holes his shirt is clean as the pain fades away quickly.

I'm, I'm uhh" he stutters in a hoarse tone. "I'm okay, I'm okay. He must have missed me in the storm and all."

Bode looks at Grady then out the window at the mysterious rider with a burning glare.

"I knew it!" said Whalen. "He knew I was fixing to get Denis! That villain ain't gonna let anyone leave until he gets what he came for and that's you, Bode, so what are you gonna do?"

Bode shifts his gaze sharply to meet that of Whalen's. He grits his teeth because he knows what is about to happen.
It is a play, acted out many times before in his sleep.

First, everyone on his side. Now they just want to feed him to the lions. It is coming. It is the predictable, the quick and easy betrayal from people who just moments ago called him their friend.

His heart beats so fast that he fears it might burst out of his chest. His jaw aches and his throat is dried out, his tongue thickens. There is a sickness embittering in his belly. Yes, he knows its coming and he does not have to wait long.

"Yes, what are you gonna do, Bode?" asks Cross.

"Yeah, Bode, this fella's got it out for you, now I don't plan on eating lead on account of some disagreement between you and him. You know I am your friend. Hell, you saved my ass back a month ago when Desmond was gunning for me with them rustling my cattle.

Bode, now dammit this ain't right You gotta make it right, whatever it is, you gotta make it right." said Randy Reeder.

"What is wrong with you people?" said Mica in a horrified pitch. "What do you want him to do? Just give himself up to that man out there?" asked Mica. "That man wants to kill him!"

"We don't know that for sure, Mica," said Cross in a condescending manner.

"He tried to kill Grady, and all he wanted to do was to leave the saloon!" she yelled back.

Meanwhile Bode sat there staring out into the darkness at the stranger. Sweat began to form on his brow as he tried to come up with an answer to just who this mysterious rider was.

"Bode!" screams Mica, her panicked voice startling him back to the moment.

"Alright!" he shouts back at her. "Alright, I'll go and see what he wants."

Bode grabs his hat and cinches it down snuggly on his head. As he made his way toward the door, his eyes meet Mica. No words needed to be said but she did anyway. "Be careful, Bode I love you!" she said.

He pauses at the door before exiting through it to the boardwalk. The wind thrashes and swirls around him. He attempts to shield his eyes from the stinging sandstorm as he slowly walks toward the edge of the boardwalk. He sees the black figure sitting calmly upon his steed.

STEELE CREEK

He appears to be watching Johnson's approach. Johnson stops and hollers out to the stranger over the wind's howl.

"I'm Bode Johnson! What do you want?"
There was an eerie silence from the stranger. He shifts in his saddle, drawing his six-gun from its holster and laying it across his saddle horn. It seemed to shine in the swirling darkness. Then he spoke.

"Drowning Creek," he said in a voice harsh and sharp enough to cut through the whistling wind.

"What?" asked Bode as if he had not heard what the man said? However, Bode did hear him, plain as day and another series of horrific and tragic memories flashed through his mind. Bode tried to clear his mind when the stranger spoke again.

"San Verde"

The name reverberated through his brain. Bode places his hands either side of his head trying to hold out the sounds. The man speaks yet again with a perfect clarity to his menacing voice now.

"San Pedro."
"Canyonville"
"Twin Buttes"
"North Fork."
"Rivers Crossing."

Each town's name slams into Bode's head with a rush of evil memories. The stranger keeps reciting the names like a judge listing off charges against a condemned man.

"No. . ." Bode said through gritted teeth.
It continues,
 "Sand Gulch."
 "Bodieston."
 "Beulaville."

"No!" Bode shouts in a louder tone still drowned out by the howling wind.

"Independence."

"Rio Rojas."

"Cahaba."

"Piedmont."

"Pleasure Beach."

"NO!" screams Bode as he staggers backwards towards the saloon doors.

The stranger turns his steed slightly, now facing Johnson. The stranger levels his six-gun at Bode. The lawman's eyes are now wide with terror. The stranger speaks only one more name. . .

"Thurmond"

Another man now is riding down the street mixed in the swirling sand he also is hidden by the sandstorm, just a shadowy figure.

The storm behind him is gone, the sun is shining and there is stillness and calm.

CRACK!

Flame shoots from the barrel of the first stranger's silver Colt .50 Bode clutches his chest and falls backwards crashing through the saloon doors and onto the floor inside, the smell of his flesh, burning his warm blood pooling on the floor is sticky.

"Bode!" shrieks Mica as she runs to his side.

"I'm hit! I am hit! I am…" Bode yells as he grabs at his chest, searching for a wound but finding… Nothing. What the hell?"

No one else had noticed the blood that had been there covering his shirt and pooling on the floor. It was gone before they could see it there.

Old Man Whalen spoke the words everyone else was thinking.

"What the hell did he want? He asked."

Bode collected himself and wiped the sweat from his forehead. His mind raced as the stranger's words kept hammering through his thoughts. The names were those of towns, towns that Bode Johnson knew all too well. They were towns where he had left his bloody trademark and calamity in his wake. He is brought back to reality by Bill Fortin's concerned voice.

"Bode; you look white as a ghost. What did he say to you?" he inquired.

Bode draws in a deep breath as he stared at the doorway. He slowly gets to his feet and straightens himself out.

"Johnson, what in the blue blazes did he say to…?"

Whalen does not get to finish his sentence before Bode abruptly cuts him off.

"He didn't!" Bode spit the words out like poison. "He didn't say anything."

"He must have said something because we could hear you talking back to him!" Whalen shot back. "What the hell did he say Bode?"

"He didn't say a damned thing, Whalen!" Bode shot back, quickly turning to face the old man with a look of forceful conviction. "He just sat there, staring at me."

"Did you recognize him?" asks Mica.

He thought hard about the stranger's face but all he could make out was his eyes. Those white eyes seemed to stare straight into his troubled soul.

"No. . . His face was hidden, a black rag over it." He replied staring out the window again.

"So he didn't say anything, nothing at all?" asks Reeder.

"Nothing!" answered Bode, remembering just how easy it was to lie to people. "He didn't say a…"

He is interrupted by that same deep baritone voice from outside now pulsating through the busted doors.

"Byron Moody"

All eyes immediately fixate on the figure outside.

Grady, his eyes wide with dread, cocks his head trying to hear.

"I heard it too." Mica said.

"Diego Teague."
"Did he just . . . speak?" asked Cross.

"He sure did!" said Reeder excitedly.

"Emmitt Duncan." The names kept coming clear and loud, now emanating through the walls.

"What? "How could anyone hear a thing especially with all that wind making such an awful racket out there?"

"No sir, I heard him myself that time, Bode Johnson!" said Whalen licking the beer foam from his moustache. "He's yapping alright. But what in Sam Hill is he yapping about is the question?"

The voice spoke again.
"Rayford Smith."
"I heard him that time for sure!" said Bill Fortin excitedly.
"Gale Monahan"

"You just think you hear something?" bellows Bode.
"No, Bode," Mica said calmly, "I heard him too. He said "Gale Monahan"

The voice speaks again.
"Clavin Register."
"Reyes Keefe."
"Homer Login"
"Hey, I knew a Homer Login!" Whalen chimes in. "He was killed a quite few years back in Arizona. He got himself kilt by some hired gun over some gold stake or

something I think."

Bode turns from the group, his pulse now pounding at his temples.

"Why is he calling out those names?" Mica asks with worry in her tone.

"Stop it . . . stop it. . . STOP IT!" shouts Bode at the figure through the large window.

CHAPTER 27

Judgement Day

Beads of sweat began to form on Bode's brow. He blinked hard as if not wanting to see what was before him. The stranger's voice continued its mysterious role call.

"Those are the names that hired gunman is Wanted for gosh you know... ugh what was his name? It was on the Poster?" said Fortin.

"That fella's name is right on the tip of my tongue, gab dammit," rattles Whalen. "We had his wanted poster for years till it turned all yella and fell apart."
"What do these names mean, Bode?" asks Mica. "Who are they? What do they have to do with us? With you?"
"I don't know, Mica," Bode said unconvincingly.

"What is all this about?" asks Reeder to no one in particular. "It doesn't make any sense that stranger out there just spitting out names!"
"They're all dead, Grady, that's the thing they all have in common" said Cross, "Bode! Like Mica said what do they have to do with us or more specifically with you?"

Bode took the gun from its holster on his left hip and stares down at the cold steel in his hand.
Bode looks up from his gun and straight into the eyes of

Mica.

"Oh Bode," cries Mica, tears in her eyes now.

"What was his name . . . ? Jon. . . ., Jonny . . ., no, David . . ., damn my cursed memory," mumbles Old Man Whalen, standing in the background, oblivious to the current conversation. He continues to mumble out names. "Billy…, Bill…"

Bode returns the gun back to its holster. All the worry and confusion is now totally gone from his face. His face is now a visage of cold, uncaring indifference. This is a different man now standing in front of the group.

They all look out to the east at the dark figure on the horse and at the other man riding up the street towards them.
The storm is disappearing behind the second man as he rides up behind him it is clearing.

There is a sudden and calming feeling that washes over Bode. He draws in a deep breath and rights his posture to a more erect stature. He feels all the stress dissipate throughout his body. His heart rate begins to slow and a very faint smile creases his lips. There was a certain familiarity with what he was now experiencing. He slowly draws the pistol from his right hip holster.

"Ah-ha! I remember now!" said Whalen "The killer's name was "Ricky Gibson."

Johnson is now calmly standing with his eyes fixed on the revolving chamber of his gun as he slowly loads bullets from his gun belt into the weapon.

"Yes sir, that's right, Ricky Gibson!" said Whalen happily.

"I've heard of that name before!" said Grady Gaston, searching his memory for details. 'San Verde,' Ricky

Gibson, which is what they called him. He was supposed to have killed three men, a woman and a kid in a shoot out up in San Verde, Oklahoma in '62." said Grady.

"That's the fella alright" fires Whalen with a stern look of disapproval.

They all look again to the window as the second rider approaches the first the wind slows its swirling.

Mica turns her head in disbelief at what she sees.

Bode paused, his eyes narrowing at the painful image in his mind. And at the site of the second horseman out there in that burning, unforgiving sand."

There was a long awkward silence. Bode could feel each of them judging him. All he had wanted was a fresh start. A break to make amends for the sins of his past, a pardon of the soul and redemption of his spirit.

Nevertheless, Bode Johnson knew all too well how this would play out. He now pulled the six-gun from its holster on his right hip. He rolled the chamber over the back of his hand, making sure each chamber was filled with a bullet. He spun the chamber quickly and then slid the gun back into the holster.

He glanced over at Mica.

"It's okay. I know how this play ends. You all feel like you do not really know me now. Well that stranger out there! He sure seems to know me. He knows where I have been and what I have done. He has probably been following me for years and now he has followed me here. Make no mistake about it; if he is here to kill me, he will find me an unwilling soul. He probably expects the same thing of me that you all expect and that is for me to turn tail and run away again. Maybe try and outrun the shadows of my past, scurry and hide in another town with another crowd of self-righteous people who will quote the Good Book but just cannot seem to live the words. Well I want you all to know something right here and now."

Johnson shifts his eyes from the group to the figures outside.

"I ain't living that way anymore. I am not afraid of you knowing who I am and I am not denying what I have done. Despite all that I'm still the man who's been to your house for supper, who's helped build your barn, a man who's been there when you needed a friend."

"I am Ricky Gibson!"

He looks into Mica's tear-filled eyes.
"I am still the man who would give you anything for the kind of life he'd only ever dreamed of. I have changed, I am bode Johnson now?"

Mica shies back, turning her face away. Bode sighs in abject heartbreak. He then clears his throat, sets his jaw in a clench and tightens his gun belt

"Well, fine then. The plain truth is that man out there is probably here for revenge or money or both and he will not settle for anything less. I can face that because I have faced death by the gun dozens of times before. However, that is not all of it. Just like every other bounty hunter or rented law dog that's ever trailed me, if he's of a mind to, he'll kill each one of you and feel justified in doing so just to get to me."

Bode was obviously nervous as he turns and heads toward the door. He pauses and looks back at the group and finally to Mica. The brief sadness in Bode's eyes is gone now, replaced by steely look of determination. Now he speaks in a calm and resolute manner. It is the pattern given to a gunman of deliberate and deadly action.

"I can't allow that to happen," he said. "So I've got a choice to make. I either run, risk that stranger killing all of you in his hunt for revenge, just as he almost killed

Grady." The group all stiffened at the paralyzing thought.

"I am going to walk through these doors, face this part of my past and end this once and for all, one way or the other," he said as he cinches down his hat and opens the door, he speaks once more as he opens the door. "Humph, guess it ain't much of a choice really. But whoever he is, he's got one hell of a fight coming to him because I sure as hell ain't running any more."

The door shuts behind him. Mica dashes to the window and shouts his name. The rest of the group follows her, finding a vantage point to view the grim event.

The windswept sand bit like a nipping coyote at Bode Johnson's face and stinging his eyes, walking to the edge of the boardwalk, shielding his eyes as he makes his way! He stops on the step and hollers to the stranger.

"You wanted Bode Johnson or should I say, Ricky Gibson, mister?" shouts Bode standing defiantly on the boardwalk. "Well here I am!"

Bode slowly descend the creaky wooden steps and makes his way along side the rider stopping at about ten feet away from him.

"I know you know who I am!" yells Bode over the roar of the sand-swept wind.
Johnson thinks he hears a discernable chuckle from the mysterious man, and takes a few more steps closer hoping to see who the man is.

"I also know you came here to kill me!"
Johnson is now at about eight feet away from the stranger.

"Well stranger . . . there's one other thing I know. . . "

CRACK!

A shot rings out from the boardwalk in front of the saloon. It is Old Man Whalen, his pistol raised at the figure. Behind him stand the others, guns at the ready, Johnson allows himself a brief smile before yelling at the mob.

"Get the hell back inside! This ain't your fight!"

"We're with ya, Johnson! Just say the word and we'll cut this egg-sucking dog down to size right here!" shouts Whalen!

"NO! Get back inside now! This is MY fight!" growls Johnson motioning the group back inside.

The group reluctantly moves back into the safe haven of the saloon. All eyes now shift to looking out the large picture window in the front. Mica said a silent prayer. The stranger sharply turns his attention to the window, his blank stare focused on Mica.

CRACK!

A shot is fired into the air by Johnson to get the stranger's attention.

"I am over here, you yellowbellied coward! This is between you and me! Now get off that horse and let's finish this!"

The stranger snaps his gaze back to Johnson. His eyes seem to narrow. He then dismounts slowly and takes a position in front of his ebony steed. His gate and stance were oddly familiar to Johnson. He somehow knew the mannerisms of the stranger as if he had seen them before. Suddenly the rider speaks in his gravelly voice.

"It is time!"

The stranger's voice speech pattern and tone is also familiar and seems to cut through the wind like a saber. Johnson stares out at his opponent trying to see his hands. Bode's own hands are at the ready, his right hand index finger again rhythmically tapping the handle of his Colt .45. He sees the stranger's eyes clearly. His stare is now focused on the stranger's right hand as it taps the handle of his own gun. A look of surprise flashes across Johnson's face quickly followed by a sly grin.

"Heh, you know . . . it's pretty funny. I knew there was something else I recognized about you! I think I just figured this whole deal out and I don't think you're gonna like the outcome of our little dance here!"

The stranger continues his tapping, as does Johnson.

"You see, now I know who you are too. Moreover, I am not scared of you anymore. You think you can come here and take away everything I have worked for, everything I have ever dreamed of in my life. Well it is not going to happen that way, my friend! Every time I have tried to lay down roots and make a good life, you would show up! I thought I could out smart you. Then I thought I could outrun you. Now I realize that I was just fooling myself. I would never be rid of you until we faced each other and settled this once and for all. Well here I am!

Today is my lucky day! Today is the day Bode Johnson begins to live his life for himself. Today is the day that I get rid of the one person who could destroy everything I had ever wanted. Today is the day you die. . . Ricky Gibson!"

The stranger's eyes open wide and flash with anger. Both men draw their guns simultaneously.

CRACK! CRACK! Two shots heard as one.

A huge streak of lightning fills the sky with a flash of brilliance as the two reports ring out together in the howling wind. Mica screams and rushes out the door and into the windswept street. She tries to cover her eyes with her hands as the sandstorm continues to swirl about. She sees a body lying in the dirt and rushes towards it.

It is Johnson.

"Bode!" she screams.

Mica drops to her knees in the dirt. She rolls him over, his Colt .45 still smoking in his hand. There is a bloodstain on his left shoulder.

"Bode!" she yells at him as if to wake the dead. "Don't you die on me? Bode"

Bode's eyelids flutter then slowly open.

"BODE! Are you alright?" she yells.

"I'm okay now, Mica," he said with a smile.

"I'm just… fine."

She pulls his head close to her and kisses his forehead. She then looks down the road to where the stranger had stood. Now he lay motionless, a dark lump in the dust-swept street, his horse standing there silently and motionless. She looks back at Bode.

"Is, is he dead?" she said, her voice trailing off.

The draft suddenly picks up in ferocity and Mica covers Bode's head and face with her apron. The wind swell builds to a crescendo then slowly dies back down. Mica lifts her head and once more gazes into Bode's eyes. They both look over to see that the body in the street is now gone. The stranger's horse has vanished into the dark wind as well.

"But … how? Where did he go?" she asks him. Bode stares out at the spot where the stranger had just tried to kill him moments ago. She helps Bode get to a seated position. Both stare down the street where the stranger once lay.

The sand storm lifts away and the air is clear the sun is bright and shining. A huge sunbeam highlights the second rider that stopped twenty feet away.

The man was dressed in a white suit, dark blue shirt and white bolo tie with a silver conch and turquoise stone in the center, sitting straight and tall riding a large white stallion.

A voice yells out from the boardwalk in front of the saloon. "Hold it," It is Old Man Whalen, his pistol raised at the figure on the White Stallion. Behind him stand the others, guns at the ready.

"Is that Gabriel?" Bill Fortin questioned.

Grady Gaston stood there in quiet disbelief. "No way possible, he died in the explosion last month. It has to be someone else!"

Bill Fortin walked out into the street towards the rider the man sits still and remained in the middle of the street sitting upon the White Stallion. Bill asks, "Are you Gabriel Samuel Horne?" There is a faint smile on the man's face as he turns his horse to the East.

"Wait." said Bill Fortin, "are you back Gabe how did you survive the blast?"

The rider trots the stallion a few feet and stops, turning back towards the group. He is now right where the dynamite exploded killing Maxwell and the others. A great burst of wind returns stirring the loose sand and dirt from the street as the man and the horse fade away, blocked once more from view by the windstorm, just as quick as the wind had stirred the sand, it died away and the street was empty again.

Only Bode Johnson, Mica, Bill and Grady are outside near the boardwalk in front of the Steele Point Diner. Mica has her arm around Bode holding him up in a seated position, "Was that really him?" she asked.

"Yes Mica, it was in fact Gabriel," he said with a calm assurance, "He has returned to help us once more, he is Gabriel but, he is not the same as we knew him before!"

Mica looks into his eyes, perplexed and hugs him tightly. The second windstorm had completely dissipated and the sands had settle down. The dark clouds continue to part, leaving the couple illuminated in the warmth of the sun's bright rays. One by one, the townspeople make their way outside and soon the street is bustling again with activity, most are oblivious to the peculiar event that had just taken place.

Mica helps Bode to his feet and they shield their eyes from the sun. The couple now stands together as one. Still, Mica wonders if what happened on that day was somehow set forth by The Almighty Himself. As for Bode Johnson, there was no uncertainty. He knew beyond shadow of a doubt that his soul had been reborn that day and with that knowledge, a comforting peace came over his being. It was the feeling of forgiveness and freedom from a lifetime of sin and suffering.

It was a feeling Bode Johnson could not wait to get used too.

CHAPTER 28

When a man holds a mirror up to his soul, what should he see? After twenty years of running gunfighter a killer as Ricky Gibson, he saw something very dark and evil. However, unlike most people with stained souls he did not try to cover it up. He decided to walk away from it entirely leaving the dark soul named Ricky Gibson alone to die out the burning sands of the Southern Texas Desert and Bode Johnson was born. However, that dark soul was not ready to give up its existence without a fight and so it tracked down its would-be killer in order to face him in one final battle for the right to live. A spiritual showdown, winner takes all.

Nevertheless, the day his sins came calling him out, well that day was very different from those of his past. On that day, the stakes were of the highest order as a troubled man would stand-alone and face his personal demon with a heart full of courage and conviction. It was indeed the showdown of a lifetime, Bode Johnson's lifetime.

For you see one soul rode out of the past, looking for revenge, while another soul desperately sought its salvation from a higher power for a brighter future.

In addition, on that day judgment was delivered through the unwavering hand and the lightning draw of an extraordinary man, whose hand was steadied by a forgotten soul, Gabriel Samuel Horne. It was a swift verdict, which saw that all participants received exactly what they justly deserved . . . and it had all happened in Steele Creek, Texas.

ABOUT THE AUTHOR

Curtis Hawk – Retired from the U.S. Army, continuing his career in County Government, retiring again in 2016.

He has been married to his wife Diane for 40 years. Together they live in in Central Illinois.

Made in the USA
Middletown, DE
18 March 2018